EMBERS
OF
HATE

PARAMOUNT SCHOOL OF ARTS SERIES
BOOK 1

SASHA-MARIE MARSHALL

Cover Design:
Sarah Hansen, Okay Creations
Editors:
Emma Moylan
Paige Lawson
Proofreader:
Emma Moylan

EMBERS OF HATE

PARAMOUNT SCHOOL OF ARTS SERIES
BOOK 1

SASHA-MARIE MARSHALL

To YAHUAH, my Father.

For those who find it difficult to forgive.

Prologue

Age 8

EVIE

"Ethan, don't call your sister a brat." Mom doesn't need to raise her voice. Her tone is enough to get our attention. "Evelyn, stop provoking your brother."

We all voted for pizza tonight except for Ethan, who wanted sushi.

Gross!

My hatred for sushi started the night Dad made us try Japanese takeout for the first time.

Tonight we made a bet on what our parents would choose for family dinner night.

I won. And Ethan's been sulking about it all night.

"Get over it." I fold my arms, frowning at him beside me in the back seat.

He sticks his tongue out and crosses his eyes.

"Mom, he's sticking his tongue out at me!" Reaching across, I smack him on the arm.

"No, I'm not, you little liar!" He does it again, then takes off his seat belt. Sliding over to my side, he pinches my thigh before I can pull it away.

"Ow! Get away from me! Mom, Ethan pinched me."

"Ethan, stop it," Mom warns. "Put your seat belt back on right now."

"But, Mom, she's lying," he whines, moving back to his seat and folding his arms across his chest.

"He's mad we didn't eat his nasty sushi. Yuck!" Triumphant, I look over to gauge his reaction. There's no way he'll do anything to me if I morph into a tail and attach myself to either Mom or Dad as soon as we get out of the van.

Annoyed, Ethan turns away from me and stares out the window. "I hate you," he grumbles. The words weren't loud enough for our parents to hear them; they were meant for my ears alone.

He knows exactly what to say to get to me.

"I hate you more!"

Dad turns to look at me, taking his eyes off the road. "Evie, don't ever say that to your brother. You never—"

"Oh my God! Eric!"

Those are the last words I hear before something crashes into the side of our van and we start spinning out of control. Glass shatters, sending shards flying. There's a persistent and sharp pain against the side of my neck. A loud screeching sound reverberates as we slide against the metal railing on the side of the road.

There's an intense ringing in my ears. My mom is screaming something, but I can't make out any of the words.

I'm tired for some reason.

My eyelids are heavy, drooping down to conceal what I can see of my brother's inert form.

My vision is blurry, and I can no longer keep my eyes open. Closing them, I succumb to the inky blackness that surrounds me.

Chapter One

Present day

SHEPHERD

I go for the usual. Hot, blonde, and easy to please. I'm not into that high-maintenance bullshit, so the girls who usually gravitate to me already know what's up.

Currently, I'm flanked by Lexie, a platinum with a banging body and a personality to match. Then there's Chase, whose name, though masculine, couldn't be more at odds with her sexy curves and lips. Lips that are currently glued to my neck, and I'm not complaining. Neither is Lexie, though I mess around with her from time to time.

What can I say?

Chicks are into me. I'm a wide receiver on Paramount School of Arts's football team, and I'm pretty easy on the eye.

Before I head into my third period class, Chase ruffles my curls where they hang over my forehead. Lexie winks at me, and they both continue down the hallway.

History.

One of the most boring subjects to ever exist.

I enter the class, and my attention immediately shifts to the back of the room. I've already scoped out the chicks in this class. Don't get me wrong, some pretty girls are in here. None have piqued my interest.

As I make my way into the room, several girls stare.

Typical.

The guys ... well, they generally glance my way unless we're acquainted.

My friends call out to me, and we slap hands before I sit down when I finally get to the back.

Dudley, on my left, is our team's quarterback. He's a giant of a guy but as soft as they come with the ladies. Dudley is the type of dude who'd marry his high school sweetheart if he had one.

John, our running back, sits to my right. He's making his way through almost every cheerleader on the team. I say *almost* because a few of the girls are playing a little harder to get.

"Hey," John says, his tone hushed as he nods his head to the left, glancing over to the front of the classroom. "We got fresh meat."

Dudley looks past me and over at John, shaking his head.

"What? I can't admire an exotic beauty when I see one?" John asks, his shoulders raised.

I look over to where he signaled, and about three seats in front, near the large classroom windows, sits a new girl.

Hmm.

She has these dark, twisty braids that fall against her back. A few of them dangle over the edge of the desk where her head is tilted forward. She's focused on writing in a notebook.

There are more than a few pairs of eyes staring her way. Still, others whisper to each other while repeatedly glancing over at her.

I frown because something about that irritates me. I mean, she's new. Shouldn't *she* be the one trying to, I don't know, look around the room to make a friend or two?

Instead, we're all sitting here like a pack of wolves, gawking at her. As if she's a queen handed to us by the benevolent gods.

Her pencil slips from her hand, and immediately, Casey, one of the guys from the swim team, dives down to swipe it up. When he hands it back to her, he hesitates, his mouth agape, as she says something to him.

Clean yourself up, man. You're drooling. I'm suffering from secondhand embarrassment over here.

I glance at John and find he's still staring at her. Chancing a look at Dudley, I notice he hasn't taken his eyes off her either. I shake my head, chuckle, then look down at my desk.

Reaching into my bag, I remove my textbook and journal. As boring as this class is, I need at least a C to ensure I get to play all my games. Coach isn't here for mediocre players. I have to keep up a solid academic record. No excuses.

Mrs. Walker comes in a few seconds later and performs her usual ritual. She removes the sum-it-up activity, replacing it with a question for our open discussion.

She faces the class and starts taking attendance. When she spots the new girl, she announces, "As you all have noticed, we have a new addition to our class this year. Evelyn Richards." Mrs. Walker gestures for her to go to the front of the class.

The girl flinches.

I smirk, finding some sick satisfaction from her discomfort.

She rises from her seat, then walks to Mrs. Walker. Lips pursed, she faces the class.

She stands a head taller than our teacher, her twisted hair hanging below her waist. The PSA uniform she wears hardly registers as a uniform. Chick has heeled combat boots on. Her black mid-thigh socks leave a hint of leg bare between where they end and the uniform skirt begins.

"Whoa, dude. She's cute," Dudley says.

"No, bro. She's *hot*," John counters.

"Well, dear, go ahead and introduce yourself to the class. You may also add two or three things you'd like us to know about you," Mrs. Walker says.

Not looking at anyone in particular, the girl opens her mouth. She purses her lips again, then acquiesces to Walker's request.

"I'm Evelyn, and I'm a transfer." She looks through the classroom windows.

No shit, *Evelyn*.

We're a full month into the school year. We all know she's a transfer student, so that was *the* lamest intro ever. She obviously has no interest in this whole spiel. Walker should put her out of her misery and stop punishing the rest of us.

"Anything *else*?" Walker asks, and I swear the girl sighs.

She freaking *sighs*.

I scowl.

"You can call me Evie."

"*You can call me Evie*." I don't realize I've mocked her out loud until the whole class turns to look back in our direction.

I glance over at John to find him eyeing me, his forehead creased in a *"Dude, what the hell?"* expression. When I look back at Evelyn to gauge her reaction, she glances away, her face unreadable. Man, what I wouldn't give to find out what she's thinking right now.

She slides back into her seat. Throwing her hair over one shoulder, she returns her attention to the notebook.

Curious, I narrow my eyes when I notice something on her neck, where her hair no longer covers it. I can't see it too well, but there's a scar on the right side. It's a raised line just above the collar of her shirt. I stare at it, moving my head forward and trying to get a better look.

A few seconds pass, and I realize what I'm doing. Frowning, I immediately bring my attention back to my textbook.

Some minutes go by, and I'm confused when I find myself glancing over at her again.

My attention shifts to Casey when he slips her a piece of paper, leaning over to whisper something to her.

She smiles at him.

I chuckle, then look away.

Throughout class, she and Casey continue passing notes. He pays zero attention to anything Walker says all period.

I don't want to be a jerk, but I can't help it when I nudge John to get his attention. "Hey, dude, watch this," I say, nodding in Casey's direction. Cupping my mouth, I yell, "Hey, yo, Casey! Get a room!"

A few girls snicker, and the guys near us laugh. Some of them noticed the exchanges between the two. The tops of Casey's ears redden, and my eyes slide over to Evelyn.

Chick reaches into her jacket pocket and pulls out a

phone. Her fingers move across the screen, and then she hands it to Casey.

He looks down at it, and back up at her like he's died and gone to heaven.

What the hell?

Casey takes out his phone, programs something into it and then hands her phone back. I know he sends her a text because she also starts tapping away.

"Will someone please remind Casey we aren't allowed to have our phones out in class?" I ask, loud enough for Walker's ears.

Douche meet *bag*.

Walker turns from the whiteboard and trains her gaze on Casey. "Mr. Walters, you know the rules, young man. Do I need to remind you of them?"

"No, ma'am." He pockets his phone and turns to Evelyn.

I don't know what he whispers to her, but whatever it is, it's got her smiling at him again.

The fingers of my right hand start drumming against my desk.

I look up at the clock on the wall to my right, hoping the last few minutes of the class drain so I can get the hell out of here.

EVIE

I hang back after class ends, waiting for the room to empty out. I have study hall next, then lunch, so I'm not rushing to leave.

Casey is waiting too.

I groan inwardly. I didn't intend to get his hopes up, because I'm not interested in anything romantic. My actions during class stem from a distaste for people who try to make others the butt of their jokes. The guy in the back and his group of friends ooze that type of personality. I'm relieved when they're among the first to leave class.

"Hey, don't worry about Shepherd. He doesn't usually act like that," Casey says when he notices me glancing over at the guy's retreating form.

I smirk. "Oh, I'm not worried."

I'm not.

I gave Casey my number because he was nice to me, and that jerk was trying to mess with him. I didn't miss how he'd mocked me either.

Class empties, leaving only a few stragglers standing around in conversation. I swing my bag over my shoulder and stand.

"You transferred from a public school?" Casey gets his stuff and falls into step beside me. I said as much in the notes we exchanged.

We stroll down the column of seats toward the front of the classroom. I'm about to answer, when a girl about my height steps in our path.

"Hey, I'm Tiffany." She has long, thick chestnut hair and friendly dark eyes.

I immediately smile.

"Listen, girl. I love how you handed Shepherd his ass today. I've never seen anyone flat out ignore him like that." When neither Casey nor I respond, she continues, "Well, anyway, can I walk with you guys? What's your next class?"

"I have PE so I'm headed to the locker rooms," Casey answers.

"Study hall," I reply.

"Seriously? Me too!" Tiffany grabs hold of my arm. "I

have lunch after, then a poetry class with Mr. Vincent. We can hang out in study hall together."

"Wait. You have poetry with Mr. Vincent after lunch? I have that class." We realize how similar our schedules are, and all but forget about Casey. When he finally gets a word in, he repeats his question about my previous school.

"I went to Crystal Springs High. It's about an hour or so south of here."

"Never heard of it." He shrugs.

"Well Georgia's pretty big," Tiffany offers.

Paramount School of Arts is in the northeastern tip of Georgia. Crystal Springs is more south, a little west of Marietta, my hometown.

"This is my turn." Casey nods and veers off in the direction of what I assume are the locker rooms.

Tiffany and I continue talking as she leads us into this huge room with a Study Hall sign posted above antique wooden doors. She pushes through ahead of me.

"Whoa." My eyes trail up brick walls that reach to a height of about fifty feet. "*This* is study hall?" I swear the place looks like a government building. It's circular in shape with high ceilings and a skylight, complete with rows of open study booths, green banker's lamps atop them.

PSA sure spends a good coin making sure it lives up to the prestige of its name. I hadn't been able to tour before transferring here, but this place has been pretty impressive so far. It's reminiscent of an Ivy League with a lofty, brown-stoned edifice. The campus is huge, stretching at least three football fields in length. Some buildings are four stories high.

"Let's sit over here," Tiffany suggests, nodding to an area with two empty chairs.

I follow her over to one of the middle rows, and we pull

out our laptops. My teachers haven't assigned me much since I'm new, but I like to be ahead rather than play catch-up when the real work begins.

"About Shepherd, he's one of the best players on our football team," Tiffany whispers, bringing my attention to her. "He's the center of attention everywhere he goes. Girls salivate over him."

I have zero interest in talking about the guy, so I steer the conversation away from him. "So where're you from?"

She frowns. "I'm from here. My mom's part Russian, and my dad's half French. Why do you ask?"

"I picked up a Latina vibe from you for some reason."

She laughs. "Well, my brother's wife is from Venezuela. They visit us often since they live so close by. I hang out with her from time to time, so maybe ...," she trails off, tongue-in-cheek.

"That's hilarious."

"How about you? Where's your family from?"

"My dad has Afro-Panamanian ancestry, and my mom is from Colombia. I was born here, though."

"That's cool. By the way, I *love* your hair. It's so freaking gorgeous. I wish my hair could do all that." She twirls her hand around as she points to my twists.

"Thanks," I say, getting distracted as I spot a Michael B. Jordan look-alike entering the room. "*Wow*. Who's he?"

She turns to the door. Whirling back around to face me, she whispers, "That's Jones. He's a football player, and he's also close friends with Shepherd."

You've got to be joking.

I fix Tiffany a vacant stare. "You know what, I don't even want to know."

Tiffany laughs and starts getting her work out.

Refocusing my attention, I look through the syllabus for

English literature. I have an extension on an essay due this Friday, but I won't need it. I plan on turning the paper in before the week's out.

Throughout the rest of study hall, we work quietly. Afterward, we grab lunch and eat it out by the field.

I get through my poetry lecture without incident. But things change when I get to my English lit class and find the Jones guy front and center. Some girls are talking to him.

As I walk by, I try to brush past them but hear, "Hey, Evelyn." I pause mid-step and turn, twisting myself around to face them.

They all stare at me.

"How do you know my name?" I ask.

"Heard it mentioned here and there," Jones replies.

OK.

"I saved a seat for you," he says, indicating the vacant chair to his right.

My mind tries to process all this. My subconscious screams at me to reject his offer, telling me any friend of that Shepherd guy is no friend of mine.

He grins, and the twin dimples appearing in his cheeks catch me completely off guard.

This guy.

My fascination with him gets the better of me. "That was nice of you, thank you." I glance at the two girls now deadpanning me.

"Excuse my manners. I'm Jones." He holds out his hand in greeting.

I shake it, then sit in the seat he'd *saved* for me.

"How'd you know I'd be in this class?"

"I have my ways." He grins before answering me for real. "Nah, I'm playing. This school is like a game of telephone. What one person knows, everybody else is bound to find out."

When he says that, I frown. The only two people who *know* my class schedule are Casey and Tiffany. Tiffany had been with me since we left history, so it couldn't have been her.

That leaves Casey.

This gives me a reason to keep myself guarded around him. There's nothing more unattractive than a guy who talks too much.

"Good to know." Better to have found this out sooner than later.

He eyes me quizzically.

"What is it?"

"You don't seem—never mind," he replies, cutting himself off and shaking his head.

"No, tell me."

"I don't get a *stuck-up* vibe from you at all. You actually seem pretty chill."

Is that what people were saying about me? I've said no more than ten words out loud today in all my classes combined.

Jones must have seen my shock because he quickly adds, "They're getting used to you. People who don't know you tend to make assumptions about your character. I should know."

When he says that, I flinch. I judged him when Tiffany told me who he's friends with.

"For what it's worth, you seem like a pretty decent guy to me," I admit.

"Thanks. That's the first time I've heard that in a while."

"Really? How come?"

"I've been a football player since I started at this school. I can't tell you how often people assume I'm a player or how often I get approached by girls, thinking I'm an easy lay."

Everything he says makes sense.

We continue talking before the teacher starts class, and Jones offers to walk me to PE when it's over. I try to remember the school's layout, but since PE is on the opposite side of campus, I'm a little lost.

"Hey, what's your number?" Jones asks.

"You don't waste time," I tease.

He laughs, and I can't help but laugh along with him. We exchange numbers and social media handles. Our interaction flows so well. It's like I've known him for way longer than a mere hour.

He drops me off and heads to his next class.

When PE is over, I realize my first day went pretty well, and I can admit to looking forward to school tomorrow.

"So, how's the new school? Made any friends today?" Dad asks as I climb into his truck from the car line.

It's been his usual habit ever since I was little. He always asks me how my day went whenever he picks me up. Of course, he'd ask now, because of the transfer. We moved to upstate Georgia about a week ago after my parents opened a bigger branch of their IT company.

My family doesn't come from money, but we were never poor either. We were always somewhere near the upper middle class, at least until my dad built his own IT business a few years back. Mom was right there in the trenches with him. Sometimes I'd come home from school and be alone in an empty house until the early morning hours. I never complained because they made it up to me on the weekends.

Every Saturday, without fail, we still go out for dinner

as a family. We keep it a priority in honor of my brother, Ethan. Whenever anything threatens the tradition, we hold to it like a lifeline.

"Today was good."

During the ride home, I tell him everything that happened during school. Excluding, of course, the bits about the guy from my history class.

Chapter Two

EVIE

"Full disclosure," Jones says, winking at me. "I peeped that you'd be coming here last week when I was in with administration."

Our teacher explains the importance of events that occur during an author's life. He goes into further detail on how they often influence their work.

I give Jones the face that tells him he's about to be a distraction again. Then I actually think about what he said. How familiar is he with the people in the office for him to get that kind of information?

"Evie, no," he says, surmising my thoughts. "I don't have that kind of pull. I was waiting for Coach when I happened to overhear a conversation a couple of teachers were having. I remember them mentioning an Evelyn. Thought the name was pretty dope and didn't think much else until people were talking about you."

"I'm not even going to bother asking what people were saying about me."

"It doesn't matter anyway. You're a cool chick, easy to be around, easy to talk to, smart—"

"Alright," I laugh, taken aback. "Lay it on, why don't you?"

"It's true," Jones adds. "Yeah, it's only been a few days, but I can tell. I have a good read on people."

"Thanks. You're not so bad yourself," I respond, tongue-in-cheek.

"OK, whatever." When he smiles, those dimples of his go on display, and I can't help but smile in return.

"Am I going to have to separate you two?" This question comes from Mr. Fritz.

"Oh, my bad, Mr. Fritz. But I do have a question, though. What happened during 1984 to prompt the author to write that kind of book?" Jones asks.

A few students in the class start laughing.

"The title of the book is *1984*. However, it was published in 1949."

Jones looks up in confusion. "Why would he name the book *1984*, then?"

"It predicted what the author thought 1984 would look like. Duh," one of the more active students in the class states from the other side of the room.

Jones rolls his eyes. "OK, smartass, I wasn't asking you. I asked Mr. Fritz."

The whole class is quiet, and a few people scowl at the kid.

I nudge Jones.

"What?" he asks.

"I know you didn't start it, but I don't want that kid having problems with anyone after class."

"Yeah, well, he should have shut the hell up then because he ain't Mr. Fritz," he says, sounding annoyed.

I sigh, grabbing my pencil to jot down the notes I missed.

Jones tries starting a conversation again, but I continue working and don't engage.

We're like that for the next half hour.

"Are you doing this because of what I said about that kid shutting the hell up?"

I don't answer but continue paying attention to our teacher.

"Evie, are you for real?"

In the next moment, he lets out a sigh of frustration, gets up, and walks over to the guy on the other side of the room.

"Sorry, dude, good looking out," he says, loud enough for the whole class to hear, before coming back over to his seat. "Is that better?"

I'm so shocked that he did that, my mouth is practically on the floor. "Did you do that because you wanted to? Or?"

"Thought about it. Figured it wasn't worth being on your bad side. Didn't take much out of me to apologize, so why not?" he says, shrugging it off.

"Wow." He's impressed the heck out of me with that display.

I'm pretty glad I decided not to let the company Jones keeps determine who he is as a person.

SHEPHERD

"What's up with you and that girl?" Beanca asks Jones when he reaches our table.

The four of us, including our other friend Lucas, have known each other since grade school.

Like me, Lucas and Jones are on the football team. We played junior varsity together during our first year.

Although Jones went straight to varsity our sophomore year, now that we're juniors, we're all on the same team. I'm closest to Lucas. We hang out a lot more than I do with Jones and Beanca.

Beanca is our venerated referee. When we get rowdy during disagreements, she's the one to reel us in, reminding us that we don't *actually* hate each other.

Lately, Beanca's been looking at me differently. I try to play dumb, but I can tell she's interested. She tries to be subtle about it, but I don't think she has a subtle bone in her body.

Beanca's a cheerleader, and although she would be my type, I can't see her as more than a friend. My dad has known her parents forever, so she's like a sister to me. I'm hoping this is a phase and that as quickly as the feelings came, they'll fade just as fast. The last thing I want is any awkwardness messing with the group's vibe.

Jones finally sits and glances over at the lunch line. "Who? Evelyn?"

"Yeah, you two seem really close," Beanca states, brows furrowed. "What's with that? You into her or something?"

I turn my attention to where Evelyn is collecting her tray from the cafeteria line. She's only been here a few days, but I can tell people are interested, even from where I'm sitting. Casey and the brunette from history are always with her. I guess those three are best friends now. Casey's lame ass probably wants more than that. He would never have looked at the brunette twice if this Evelyn chick wasn't with her.

Whatever.

"She's cool," Jones says to Beanca.

"She's cute," Lucas chimes in, his eyes scanning her as she sits at one of the corner tables with the others.

"She's already spoken for, Lucas." Jones is mid-bite, the burger halfway to his mouth, as he focuses his attention on Lucas.

"For real? Casey?" Lucas asks, a surprised look on his face as he glances over at Casey, who's seated next to Evelyn. "Dude wasted no time."

"Ah, no, actually. I saw her first." Jones sinks his teeth into his burger.

My gaze flashes from Jones back over to where Evelyn's sitting. She sits wide-eyed at something the brunette is saying. Then Casey says something that has the three laughing among themselves.

Jones hadn't been the one to see her first. Casey was. The fact that he's trying to stake some kinda claim on her is so dumb I almost feel inclined to comment on it.

I don't, because who cares about this chick anyway?

I get it. She looks good, but there are lots of other hot girls here.

"Jones, she's been here less than a week." Beanca brings my attention back to the conversation. She gives Jones a quelling look.

He shrugs. "I'm a simple guy, Bee. I see a fine girl. I talk to her. And when I find she's cool, I want her."

"I can see it," Lucas agrees, looking from Jones and then over to Evelyn.

I frown. Is this the chosen topic of conversation for lunch?

If so, I'd rather pass.

"Hey, I, uh, gotta talk to Green before fifth period starts, so I'll catch you guys later." I stand, giving them the bullshit excuse so they don't bust my chops for leaving them hanging. The last thing I want to do is sit around talking about some chick.

I mean, I have nothing against Evelyn. The past few days haven't been the best. I've been feeling off. I'm assuming it's because of Coach. He's been brutal lately due to football season starting soon.

"Shep, you barely ate anything," Beanca points out.

Lucas hops up and picks up his tray. "Dude, I'm coming with. Green had the nerve to give me an F for my solar system project. Said my dome earth theory has no place in academia. I swear, these teachers and their one-sided view of what they *think* reality is, is what's wrong with education."

"I wasn't hungry," I tell Beanca, ignoring Lucas's comment. Nodding to both her and Jones, I turn and leave the table.

Lucas falls into step beside me. "So what do you really think of the new girl?"

"Dude, it's whatever." I shrug off his question.

"You have to admit she's pretty hot."

"Did you follow me out here just to talk about her?"

"Uh ... no, but we *can* talk about what's gotten you so pissed. What's up?"

"Green," I grind out.

"You and me both. Woman's got a real stick in the wrong place."

I come up with some excuse to go to my car, telling Lucas I forgot something.

We part ways, and when I get to the parking garage, I park my ass on the stairs and pull out my phone.

Evelyn Richards.

I type her name in the search bar on Our Social. We have Jones as a mutual friend, making it easy to spot her among the other results under the same name.

Private.

I do a quick check of another one of Jones's social media accounts and find her under the username *evelyn8luv*.

Private.

I have no idea why I'm trying to find info on her but in the next few minutes, I search for her on other platforms.

Nothing.

I don't notice anyone behind me until small hands push their way around my torso.

"Hey, hottie," Lexie whispers, her hair falling over the shoulder of my jacket.

I stand and turn to face her, moving the phone to my side.

Lexie looks smoking hot today, her body filling out in all the right places.

"Hey," I say, pocketing my phone.

"What are you doing out here?" She anchors her hands at my sides. She's standing one step up from me, so we're nearly nose to nose.

"Nothing exciting."

"I know how we can *make it* exciting," she suggests, sliding her hands to the lapels of my jacket and tugging me into her.

We start kissing and she's got her hands all in my hair, chest pressed to mine, and *damn*. I get lost in the attention she's showering me with.

"My car's over here, Evie. Oh—," someone says.

Lexie continues making out with me, not caring that we have an audience.

"What is it?" I hear Evelyn's voice before I see her. Then she steps into view next to the brunette.

Lexie continues devouring my mouth. The other girls can't see her face, but her hair doesn't conceal my profile.

Evelyn turns to investigate what's caught the brunette's

attention. When her eyes finally land on me, I have the oddest reaction.

Instead of letting up, I put my hands in Lexie's hair, framing her face. I don't know what the hell's come over me, but I close my eyes and deepen the kiss, giving Lexie as good as she's giving.

When we finally end the kiss, my eyes move to where the girls are, but I find the place empty. I scan the surrounding area and still find no sign of them.

"Were you waiting for someone?" Lexie asks, getting her mirror out and fixing her hair.

"No," I reply, distracted, and feeling at odds with myself.

I'd *wanted* Evelyn to see us. Some sadistic part of me craved it. She's only been here for a few days, and ever since that first day in history, her attitude has grated on my damned nerves. She's the new kid on the block. She doesn't get to ignore us and expect everyone to go after her, like dumbass Casey and now Jones.

Not happening.

"Hey, I need to get to class," I say, shaking myself from my thoughts.

"Yeah, me too. Continue this later?"

"I'll let you know." I jog to my fifth period. I'm sure class has already started, judging by the lack of students roaming the hallways,

Shit.

Green is gonna cane my ass.

Chapter Three

EVIE

Since I've been at PSA, I've seen Shepherd hook up with at least two different girls. And those are only the ones I know of.

It's been less than two weeks.

Even the girl in his group of friends looks like she's ready anytime he says go.

I don't care how attractive a guy is or how popular. There's nothing cute about hopping between girls like they're toys. There's a term for guys like that.

Messy.

I don't know why I'm surprised. Guys like Shepherd live for attention. Couple his looks with the fact that he's a star athlete, and you've got a guy who can't help but be full of himself. He knows he can pull girls and has no problem using them when they make themselves so readily available.

The way he'd grabbed that girl on the staircase last week, pulling her against him ...

I realize I'm still thinking about the scene they made in

the parking garage and mentally shake myself, tuning back into my poetry lecture.

I leave class with Tiffany and am heading to English lit when Jones comes up beside us.

"Hey, did you do well on that essay from last Friday?" he asks.

"Yeah. Why, what's up?" I wave to Tiffany as she heads off to class.

"I'm in serious need of a tutor." He punctuates this statement by holding up his essay. There's a D- inked in blue at the top of the paper. "What did you get?"

"An A."

"I *knew* you'd pull an A."

I'm about to ask how he could know that, but I offer to help him instead. "I can tutor you if you want. I'm good for Wednesdays or Thursdays."

"Wednesday nights work for me," he replies. "Is seven good with you?"

"*Ooh*, no. That's a little too late. How about five?"

"Perfect. Your place or mine?"

"Doesn't matter. My parents trust me, so as long as they at least have the address of the place and the necessary names, I'll be good."

"They're that cool?"

If the relationship I have with my parents is a little different than the average teenager's, it's because of losing Ethan. We got closer after that. We had to delve into deeper topics than most eight-year-olds are accustomed to. The trauma of the whole ordeal forced us to be raw in conversations, which continued through the years. My parents and I tell each other everything. Well, almost everything.

"Yeah, they're *that cool*," I say, emphasizing his words.

"Let's have it at your place then."

I shrug my acceptance and smile as he nudges me before we enter our classroom.

Hours later, when school dismisses, I head to the car line and wait for my dad to pick me up.

A few minutes go by as I'm standing by the curb when I sense someone watching me. I usually keep my eyes averted in situations like this because I don't care who stares. Once I learned I couldn't stop them, it was pointless to care.

Against my better judgment, I look up and over to the iron gates where cars are leaving. I recognize Shepherd standing behind the wrought iron fence, staring back at me, his expression cold.

I immediately look away. It doesn't take long for me to process that he's not a car rider. He's out of place here.

I don't look back over at him. And when my dad finally arrives, I hop in his truck, completely ignoring Shepherd.

I refuse to let that guy get to me.

We get home, and I help dad prepare for the small party of people that'll be over at our house tonight. He's signed a contract with a local company to handle all its IT and technical services. The company has a large infrastructure, and the contract will prove lucrative.

I shower and change into a black halter dress that reaches mid-thigh. The top half of my back is bare, with only a bow knot present at the base of my neck. I throw on a pair of matching strappy heels before heading downstairs.

"Oh, sweetheart, you look lovely," Dad says.

I walk over and kiss his cheek before checking the table settings one last time. Since it's a school night, I'm not expected to clean up, but he does want me to stay until our guests leave.

When the first few people arrive, I greet and usher them into the living room where my dad is.

About ten guests later, I decide to pull the door closed. Dad told me there would be twelve people total, and it's already twenty minutes past the set arrival time.

I strike up a conversation with a handsome guy named Tony, who seems more than a few years younger than my dad. He's in the middle of describing some new tech he's interested in when the doorbell rings.

Some of the other guests surround Dad, so I excuse myself.

I'm smiling when I overhear my dad's laughter, but then I open the door and immediately deflate.

Standing on the doorstep in front of me … is Shepherd.

I'm so shocked to find him there that several seconds pass before I realize he's not alone.

Next to him is an older dark-haired woman. His mother, I presume, though they look nothing alike.

He looks down at me, his sardonic blue eyes daring me to look away.

I shift my gaze to the older woman. "Good evening." I smile, but it doesn't reach my eyes. Opening the door wider, I allow them in.

"Good evening. Young lady, I'm here to see Mr. Richards," the woman says, turning to face me.

"Of course. My father's right over there." I direct her attention to Dad, who's chatting with a small group of guests.

"So you *are* his daughter, Evelyn. Oh, you look beautiful, my dear," she says. "He has said such wonderful things about you."

"Thank you," I reply, hesitating because I don't know her name.

"Mrs. Buchanan, dear," she says, holding out her hand. "But you can, of course, call me Jackie." We shake hands before she turns to Shepherd. "Shep, will you do me a favor and get us a drink? I'm parched." She leaves us standing there and goes over to my dad.

I attempt to walk away but a hand reaches out, grabbing my wrist. I'm stunned by the contact, instantly pulling my wrist free from Shepherd's grasp.

"What do you want?" I ask, careless of how rude I come across. I'm under no obligation to be kind to this guy. I also don't like people touching me without my permission, least of all him.

"Where can I find something to drink?" he asks, scowling at me.

"There," I reply flatly. I point to the table of refreshments and walk away from him, returning to Tony and the conversation we were having.

When a few minutes pass, I chance a glance behind me to find Shepherd glaring at me. He shifts his gaze and walks to the other side of the room.

He looks different tonight. Definitely not like he does at school. I'm sure it's because of the blue button-down and black slacks he's wearing. Dressed like this, he looks more ... mature.

Too bad he was *the* furthest thing from that.

I bring my attention back to Tony when I realize, with annoyance, that I haven't heard anything he's been saying.

We're all finally seated for dinner a half hour later. I end up between Tony and my father, who's at the head of the table. On his right, and opposite of me, is Shepherd's mother, Jackie. Next to her is Shepherd.

"It's a shame my husband couldn't come tonight," Mrs. Buchanan says to my dad at one point. "He would have been ecstatic to meet you, since you're also an avid fisherman. He'd have regaled you with stories about his fishing trips."

They mention possible future get-togethers, and I grumble under my breath.

"What was that, sweetheart?" Dad asks.

I feign a smile and tell him it's nothing.

But it's *not* nothing, damn it. The last thing I need is an obligation to spend more time in the presence of a guy with such a sour disposition.

I look over at said guy and find him smirking at me. I roll my eyes, and then he's full-on chuckling. When his mom asks him what's funny, the chuckle morphs into a cough.

Shepherd reaches for his water glass and tells her something caught in his throat.

If only.

"Dad, I'll go get dessert," I say, rising from my seat.

Dad nods.

"I can help if you can't manage." Shepherd grins up at me. "You know, like if there's a lot, or if it's too heavy."

I'm aware he only said it to get under my skin. I want to ignore him and leave the room, but I can't, not with everyone's eyes on me.

"No, that's fine," I say as politely as I can manage. "Tony here has already offered to help. We'll manage." I look down at Tony, pleading with him to confirm what I said.

Tony looks at them, then rises from the table. "Yes, of course, happy to lend a hand."

"Thank you," I say once we're in the kitchen.

"Sure." I can tell he wants to ask why I didn't accept Shepherd's offer of help. He won't though, because at least *he's* a gentleman.

I prepare the platters while he talks about IT. I'm not

well versed in all the technical terminology, but I listen anyway. Once he sees I'm done, he lifts two trays off the counter and waits for me to grab the last one.

"Evie, sweetheart, you didn't tell me Shepherd goes to your school," Dad says as I place the tray on the table.

I sigh. "He does." I nod at him and gesture to the cheesecake. "Cookies and cream are the ones in the middle." Those are his favorite, so I point them out first.

He smiles, then leans over to kiss my cheek before taking a slice.

I'm smiling as I reach for one of the Danishes on the platter. Before I get a chance to take it, Shepherd's fork spears it, and he brings it over to his plate. He then reaches out lightning fast and takes the other one.

I'd only placed two cheese Danishes on the platter by our side of the table, and he'd taken them both.

If I show that what he did bothers me, he'll feel like he won. So instead, I turn to Tony, leveling him with one of my most radiant smiles.

"Tony, could you please place one of the cheese Danishes from that platter over there on my plate?" I place my dessert plate in Tony's proffered hand.

After he hands it back to me, I thank him and proceed to enjoy every ... single ... bite.

Chapter Four

SHEPHERD

"**S**hep, we missed you last night."

I close my car door and walk over to Lucas, fisting the keys into my pocket.

My thoughts return to the dinner at Evelyn's place.

After football practice, a few of the players planned on going to our usual hangout in Tallulah. It's a campsite about thirty minutes north of us. Lots of nature, natural springs, and waterfalls.

I took a rain check because Jackie had asked me to fill in for my dad at a business social. I'd looked for a way to refuse because hanging out with a bunch of adults talking sales and mergers wasn't exactly my scene. She'd indicated an invitation card sitting on our kitchen island, and the name on the card had given me pause.

Mr. Eric Richards.

Eric Richards?

Evelyn Richards ...

That had to be too much of a coincidence. The guy's

face was on the invitation. And although his skin was much darker than Evelyn's, I could tell they were related.

Yesterday, I went to the carpool area after school with the intention of possibly ID'ing Mr. Richards. And sure enough, as Evelyn's ride pulled away, I got a good enough look to verify he was her father.

I relished the thought of seeing her reaction when I showed up at her house. I looked forward to it.

She didn't disappoint.

I don't know when it started, but Evelyn's discomfort has become my personal thrill.

I mean, she looked good last night. I'll give her that. Her dark eyes looked even better when she rolled them at me for smirking at her and her obvious annoyance as I stole the pastries she wanted was well worth it.

I tell myself it's because I want her to know her place, to knock her off that pedestal she's gotten on since being here. But the drive to piss her off is becoming a bad habit I can't shake. The more I feed it, the more it grows.

"Shep, did you hear me? Where'd you go?" Lucas asks, frowning at me.

"Sorry, man. I was thinking about this history paper I haven't started." It's not completely untrue. I have a history essay that I need to write, but I can't seem to put pen to paper to get it done. "What were you saying?"

"I was telling you about what you missed last night. Dude, Dudley has a secret crush on some girl. We found out because he was social media stalking her when one of the guys grabbed his phone. No one had a chance to look at her profile before Dudley dove after him. The phone ended up in the river."

"Looks like I didn't miss much."

"You have a point." He shrugs in agreement.

We get to my locker and notice heart-shaped cards held to it by lollipop magnets.

"Well, well, someone has a new secret admirer." Lucas whistles, his eyebrows dancing.

It's not Valentine's Day.

Hell, it's not even February.

This isn't the first time this has happened to me, but it's the first time there are so many. Twelve cards are pinned haphazardly all over the door of my locker.

Lucas takes one off and reads it.

Blue
B-Beautiful
L-Lovely
U-Unique
E-Enticing

He proceeds with another.

Eyes
They say they're a window to the soul
Yours have this magnetic pull
Me in until I'm full
Of you

When he finishes the third poem, he's laughing so hard that a few people look over at us. I grab the rest of the hearts from my locker and throw them in a nearby trash can.

"Duuude, those were masterpieces. Why'd you throw 'em out?" he asks, still laughing.

It's not that I don't like poetry. It's this flowery shit that's *not* my cup of tea.

Ignoring him, I grab the books I need for first period and

close my locker. That's when I notice Chase strolling toward us.

She reaches up to kiss me before turning to acknowledge Lucas.

"Hey, my parents are gone for the weekend, soooo I'm having a party at my place after the game Friday night. You guys down?" Her gaze shifts between Lucas and me.

Lucas agrees for us both when Beanca enters the hallway. Her younger sister, Beverly, whispers something to her, and then the two part ways.

Beverly is a freshman, and unlike Beanca, she doesn't like socializing much.

When Beanca reaches us, Chase extends the invitation to her. Beanca glances at where Chase is holding on to my arm. "Yeah, sure, I'll be there. I assume Jones is invited too, right?"

"For sure! Ya'll invite whoever. I only wanted to make sure my eye candy would be there." Chase punctuates this by kissing the shoulder of my uniform jacket. She looks over at Beanca. Something passes between them before Chase pats my shoulder and walks off.

"Shep, be careful with her. You don't know what kind of *diseases* she might be carrying."

"Ouch! Not nice," Lucas says as he lifts the cards up to her face.

"What are those?"

"Shep's got a new *admirer*."

Beanca shakes her head and gives me a sympathetic look. "I'll see you guys later."

After the first period ends, I spot Lexie on the way to my next class. Or rather, she spots me.

"Hey, hottie. You got any plans for tonight?" she asks, reaching up to place her lips on mine. When I don't kiss her back, she tilts her head away from me, her gray eyes searching, brows drawn together. "What's up?"

I frown because hell if I know.

I place my arms around her waist and pull her to me. "Nothing's wrong," I reply, grinning before we start making out. We don't stop until I hear a loud cough coming from behind me. Breaking the kiss, I turn my head to see where it came from.

Casey and the brunette from history stand outside the double doors leading to the third-floor classrooms. They walk by where we're standing on the landing, a few feet from the stairs.

"Don't let us interrupt, Shep," he says as they head down the stairs.

What the hell?

I release Lexie. I'm about to ask the idiot what the hell all that was about when she wraps her arms around my waist, caging me against her.

"He said he didn't want to interrupt, Shep," she complains, gliding her hands up my chest where my jacket lies open. "Besides, it looks like *he's* got his hands full these days."

"What's that?" I ask, needing her to clarify what she meant.

"Casey," she replies, distracted. "The whole swim team is talking about how he's always with that girl, Evie."

Frowning, I grab hold of her hands, removing them from my shirt.

"We'll be late if we don't get to class." I'm suddenly not in the mood. I head through the doors, and Lexie follows me, still rambling on.

"I mean, this is the most action he's gotten since we've

known him. Hey, slow down! We're not that late." She's almost running, attempting to catch up to me.

I try to ignore her.

Throughout the second period, I can't concentrate. My mind keeps going back to what Lexie said about Evelyn.

First Casey, then Jones, then that Tony guy from last night who's too old for her.

I get to history, and when I spot Evelyn, something comes over me.

She's standing by her desk, taking stuff out of her bag. I don't have to pass by her desk to get to my seat, but today I feel like taking the scenic route.

I get close enough to Evelyn, bumping into her as she's about to sit down.

The notebook she's holding falls to the ground between us.

She looks at it, then up at me. I guess she's waiting for me to apologize because she makes no move to pick up her notebook.

I raise an eyebrow, turn, then walk away. Taking a seat, I shift my eyes back over to her, and she immediately looks away.

I'll admit, I'm a little disappointed. I don't know what I thought would happen, but I didn't expect her *not* to react.

She says something under her breath, and my ears perk up, but I can't make it out.

Casey picks up the notebook, places it on her desk, then his eyes meet mine.

Where the hell did *he* come from?

He looks away and whispers something to her, placing a hand on her arm.

I look at where his hand touches her. It's a damned

notebook. It didn't break, so his attempt at *consoling* her is lame.

"Aw. Still haven't found a room, huh?" I ask.

Evelyn stiffens but keeps her focus on the front of the room … and on Casey. She smiles over at him and the two strike up a conversation as if nothing happened.

My jaw tightens.

I notice a few kids glancing at me, and I scowl at them.

"The hell are *you* looking at?" I say to one kid.

He shrugs, looking away.

I'm relieved when John and Dudley finally get here. We discuss practice and our upcoming games against a few rival teams.

"So, who is she?" I ask Dudley, bringing up his mystery chick.

"He's not gonna tell you," John repeats. "He didn't tell any of us, so what makes you think he's gonna let you in on who she is?"

Walker enters and immediately starts class, silencing all conversations.

My eyes move of their own volition to where Evelyn's sitting. She's glancing at an empty seat, and I guess the brunette either left or skipped. She was with Casey earlier.

Sucks.

I find myself thinking about Evelyn again when she's not in the cafeteria during lunch. Casey's at a table with a few kids from the swim team, but she's not with him.

Jones isn't here either.

After school, we're in the locker room changing into our gear before practice starts. "Hey, what happened during lunch today?" I ask.

"Yeah, where were you at?" Lucas adds.

Jones pulls on his shoulder pads. "I had to do some groveling with Evie 'cause I had to push our session to seven tonight." When I look at him confused, he explains that Evelyn's tutoring him for their literature class. "Anyway, I took her out for lunch to make up for the inconvenience."

"Nice." Lucas slaps him on the shoulder.

"Oh, OK. Cool," I say.

We continue gearing up.

Jones pulls on his helmet, then looks over at me. "You good?"

"Yeah, why?" I ask.

Lucas eyes me suspiciously.

"'Cause you look kinda off. If it's over Lexie, it's not worth it. You have Chase. Plus, I been told you that girl is loose. I thought you were only having fun with her."

"What? Lexie? No, trust me, I'm good." Lexie messes around. She's the last person on my mind right now.

"Alright, just checking. I'll see you out there," Jones says, exiting the locker room.

Lucas is waiting for me and I nod in Jones's direction, letting him know I'll meet up with him out on the field.

"You sure?" he asks.

"Yeah, I'll see you out there."

I reach for my gloves and start putting them on as he walks out. The left glove glides on, no problem. Then I'm trying to put the right one on, and it starts giving me shit. I yank the hell out of it, and it still doesn't want to fit right. I use my teeth to pull both it and my left glove off, throwing them on a bench close by.

I don't need them anyway.

When I get out to the field, I realize Coach doesn't look happy. So it's no surprise that we're all near death two hours later.

Practice is brutal, and I'm drenched when it's finally over.

I'm definitely going to feel the pain tomorrow, and some part of me wishes it could start now.

I come out of the showers and notice Jones is freshening up, looking at himself in the locker room mirrors.

I drag on my sweatpants and a T-shirt.

"Whoa, Jones. You got a date?" one of the guys asks.

Jones is in denim and a black tee. He snaps on a diamond stud in his ear. "You can call it that. She doesn't know it yet," he replies. "I like the challenge." He winks at us before walking out.

A few other guys leave, and after they're gone, I grab my bag, throw it over my shoulder, and close my locker. When the dumbass door bounces back at me, I slam it shut.

I head to my car and get my phone out.

I call up Lexie and ask if she wants to hang out since she mentioned it earlier. She starts explaining why she can't so I hang up and call Chase instead.

"Yeah, for sure. Where do you wanna go?" she asks.

"You wanna come over?"

And now I've got plans tonight too.

Chapter Five

SHEPHERD

We win our second football game for the season. It's against Excelsior Academy, one of our rival schools, and we crush them.

Both Jackie and my dad missed it. This was one of the first times they both couldn't make it to my game. They have their businesses to run, and sometimes my game schedule clashes with theirs. I'm good, though. Nothing can ruin my high.

We get to Chase's party and pile into her place. Cheers reverberate through the house as we enter.

Since we're all minors, the alcohol isn't shared. It's in a back room where Chase's dad keeps it.

Her parents aren't home right now, but I'm not stupid enough to drink tonight. I'm behind the wheel, so I have to keep away from the stuff. Lucas, Jones, and Beanca all rode with me after the game. We all have our own cars, but I'm the designated driver tonight.

As we walk to the back room, I notice Jones looking

around, searching for someone. He heads out the front door when he doesn't find who he's looking for.

Lexie and a few of the other cheerleaders are already in the back, and as we enter the room, she comes over to me.

"I missed you!" she says, a little louder than necessary, pulling my head down to hers.

The taste of alcohol hits me as she pushes her tongue into my mouth, and I twist away from her.

"What?" she whines, scrunching up her face.

I don't like it when chicks go overboard with alcohol. It's too early in the night, and I don't have time for this shit. Peeling her hands off my face, I distance myself from her. When she makes her way over to me again, I leave the room.

"Hey, y'all can catch me out front. It's not like I can drink this stuff tonight anyway."

Beanca follows me out, Lucas stays, and I don't know where Jones has disappeared to.

I grab two slices of pizza from the stack of boxes in the kitchen, then pull out a Coke from one of the coolers on the floor. Beanca nibbles on popcorn.

We discuss homecoming, and she asks me who I'm thinking of going with.

"Honestly, I haven't thought that far ahead," I say. "I guess I'll go with either Lexie or Chase. More so Chase."

When I voice this, she looks away and continues chewing on her popcorn.

I finish my pizza and down the Coke.

When I get back to Beanca's side after getting rid of the trash, she's staring at some point in the room, a snarl on her face. I follow her line of vision to see what she's staring at and instantly regret it.

Jones is holding Evelyn's hand as he ushers both her and the brunette chick through the crowd. They get to a set of chairs on the opposite side of the room, and then he sits next to Evelyn and starts chatting her up. The other girl looks around, realizing she's now the third wheel. And when her gaze lands on Beanca and me, she freezes.

I frown.

Hmm.

Interesting.

She then looks away, taps Evelyn, and whispers something in her ear.

Evelyn doesn't look over at us. Instead, she says something to the other chick before turning to Jones. When she's done talking, she stands and pulls the brunette up with her. Jones stands then too.

"Where are you going?" Beanca asks.

I realize she's directing the question to me, and I pause. I'd started walking over to them. "Don't you wanna know why Jones invited those two?" The question is complete bullshit, and I have no idea why I even asked it.

"Um, I already know. Are you sure *you* don't? I mean, Jones hasn't been secretive about his interest in that girl."

I don't comment.

"Whatever, let's go. I guess she'll be a part of our group anyway once Jones starts dating her." Beanca brushes past me.

When we finally get over to them, my mood has soured.

"Hey!" Beanca says with way too much excitement in her voice. "I'm Beanca. Jones is super rude for not introducing you to us, but nice to meet you." She holds out her hand to Evelyn.

Evelyn stares at her. Several seconds tick by before she glances at Jones and then reaches a hand out to Beanca. "Evelyn."

"I'm Tiffany," the brunette chimes in.

We both nod at her.

"Jones, thanks for inviting us, but we'll see you around," Evelyn says, turning to Tiffany.

"Are you leaving?" I hear myself ask.

"Evie, come on. Why?" Jones grabs hold of her hand.

I look down at where he's holding her hand. She's not pulling free or moving away from him like she did to me when I'd done the same thing to her. Something about it grates on me, and the bad habit I can't get rid of begs me to feed into it.

My hand fists against my jeans, and I can't stop myself when I say, "She's not worth it, Jones."

All three girls look up at me, but I train my eyes on Evelyn.

She masks her expression with a blank stare. Turning, she stalks out of the house, Tiffany behind her and Jones in their wake.

"Shep, what was that all about? That was completely unnecessary."

I don't want to talk about it. I don't want to do anything right now, least of all explain my actions to anyone, including Beanca.

"Jones was ... begging her to stay," I say instead. "That shit was ridiculous."

"So," Beanca counters. "That's what you do when you like somebody."

I turn away and leave her standing there because I don't want to hear about who Jones likes or who likes him.

I look up to find this sweet-looking petite chick eyeing me, and I smile at her.

Taking that as enough of an invitation, she walks over to me. "I'm Kate," she says, and then she starts flirting with me.

I try to be into it, but I'm not.

I have no idea why.

Out of the corner of my eye, I get a glimpse of Jones coming back into the house.

I'm not hearing anything the chick in front of me is saying. All the blood rushes to my head and neck at the sight of Evelyn's reentrance into the house. She's holding on to Jones's arm, leaning against him as they squeeze past the crowd near the front door. She's laughing and smiling at him when he brings his lips near her ear to say something to her.

My chest tightens, and I lose it. I look away from them and walk out of the room without a backward glance.

When I exit the back door, I slam it shut and find myself alone in the backyard.

"Damn it!"

I slam my fist against the wall, then turn to look out into the darkness. I drag my hands through my hair, taking these deep-ass breaths.

What the hell is wrong with me?

My heart is pounding. It's like it wants to come out of my chest.

I. Don't. Care!

I don't care who Evelyn's with. I don't. I don't even know her. She's just some chick playing a bunch of different guys. She can be with whomever she wants. If she chooses to be with Casey, who gives a damn? If she likes Jones. What the hell does that matter?

After several minutes pass, I open the back door and stride back into the house. I grab Chase when I see her leaving the back room and walk us into the living room. I find a spot in full view of everyone, place her back against the wall, and start making out with her.

Because I can.

When she pushes at my chest, I break the kiss, and she takes in a grateful breath.

"*Damn*, Shepherd. If you wanna go upstairs ...," she trails off, her hazel eyes darkening to almost brown.

No.

I don't want to go upstairs. I want to stay right ... here.

Turning us so I can survey the room, I grab at her waist, pulling her against me. My eyes search the room and I lean down, devouring her mouth. When my gaze finally lands on my intended target, I wait.

From where she's standing, Evelyn must sense that my eyes are on her because she slowly turns her head.

Her eyes connect with mine, and I leave her staring at me as I close my eyes and let Chase take the lead. I reopen them a few seconds later, and direct them to the spot Evelyn is still occupying.

She tears her gaze away and says something to Jones. Then the two of them gesture to Tiffany. All three walk out of the house for the second time tonight.

My phone vibrates a few minutes later, and I immediately check the screen.

It's Jones who's messaged our group chat.

Jones: Hey, I'm riding with Evie and Tiffany. I won't be back, so get home safe.

Lucas: Duuuuude. Evie's totally into you.

Jones: Yeah, we're heading to my place now.

Beanca: Wow

Jones: It's not like that, Bee.

Lucas: Suuure.

I should be happy for Jones, happy that things are moving along for him with the girl he's interested in.

But I'm not.

Does that make me an awful friend?

Probably.

Knowing I won't be much for company for the rest of the night, I tell Chase I'm leaving. She whines about all the fun I'll be missing out on, and I shrug her off before heading out to my car. I don't text Beanca or Lucas because I don't want them wondering why I'm leaving them high and dry tonight.

I wouldn't know what to say.

Chapter Six

SHEPHERD

"So Bee's been playing up to you a lot lately." Lucas pulls off his cleats, then glances at me.

I guess Beanca isn't trying to hide it. She followed me around during the first half of the party the other night. And ever since, she's been on me about wanting to hang out alone.

"That obvious, huh?" I reach for the pair of jeans I left hanging over the locker room bench.

"Well, it's better you than me." Averting his gaze, Lucas pushes his gear into this locker. "The last thing I need is an entanglement with my best friend."

Something about how he says that is off, but I don't know what to make of it. It probably has to do with Coach and his attitude during practice.

"Make sure y'all know what you're doing. Once you leave the friend zone, there's no going back." He finishes this statement with a look of annoyance. Lucas believes in keeping best friends as just that, never muddying the waters. The only thing I'm trying to figure out is where I gave him the impression that *I'd* be into playing in those waters.

"I'm sorry? Did I say I wanted anything more than friendship with Bee?"

"If you do, you'll need to drop whatever you've got going with Chase and Lexie." The way he says this is matter-of-fact. Like I'm stupid or something.

"OK, Dad. I'll be sure to take care of that right away."

When he finally realizes how he's coming off, he immediately reels himself in. "I'm sorry, bro," he states with a sigh, rubbing his neck.

"Don't worry about it. You're good. I know how it is."

"How what is?" he says, his tone sharp again.

"Keeping friendships as priority." I frown. "Dude, what's up with you?"

Lucas's brows knit together, then he throws his backpack over one shoulder. "Nothing I can't handle. I've been easily agitated lately."

"Coach? Or is it Green again?"

He contemplates and then says, "You know what? It's Green. Has to be. Dude, she knows I need to keep up a C in her class to play, and she's like Cruella de Vil messing with my grades. Remember that solar system project I was telling you about the other day? She only bumped it up to a D."

"Why not get your mom involved?" I collect my stuff, and we head out to the parking lot.

Lucas's mom is his biggest support. That woman would do anything for him. I've always envied their relationship.

My biological mother left my father and me when I was five and never looked back. My memories of her were good until they faded altogether. All except one. The one where she promised no one could or would ever come between us.

Liar.

She lied. Then she left.

"No, she's got a lot going on," Lucas responds.

"Oh yeah?"

"Nothing we can't handle. Hey, what's up with you and Jones anyway? It's like you two are avoiding each other."

I shrug. "We have a difference of opinion on the company he keeps."

"Company? Meaning Evelyn?"

I scowl in annoyance, no longer wanting to have this conversation.

"Dude, what's your problem with that girl? She seems cool, especially if she's got Jones hanging around her. You know how choosy he is. Plus, they have that literature class together. It's not like he has to go out of his way to be with her."

We're almost to our cars, and he stalls us when I make no comment, grabbing hold of my arm. "If I didn't know any better, I'd say you have a thing for this girl."

"What the hell are you talking about, Lucas, huh? I don't even know her." The notion that I feel anything like that for Evelyn is ridiculous.

"Alright, you have a point."

"You think?"

"But that leads me to question your bias against her. What's up with that?

I come up with nothing.

He narrows his eyes and surmises, "Maybe it's because Jones spends more time with her than us now. I'll admit, I've had moments where I felt annoyed at the amount of time you and Beanca spend together without us. I get it, actually." Satisfied with his conclusion, he falls back into step beside me.

Lucas is probably right. I avoid Jones sometimes because he often steers the conversation toward the subject of Evelyn. It's not like I can tell him to stop or change the subject because then he'll think something's up.

"We have the Tallulah trip tomorrow, and I'm pretty sure she won't be there. Jones said something about her always spending Saturdays with her parents," Lucas adds. "It'll be the four musketeers and everyone else."

We talk about other stuff and finish up before parting ways when we get to our cars. He climbs into his truck and waves before heading out.

I sit in my car, wondering why I'm irritated instead of feeling excited about tomorrow's trip.

Chapter Seven

EVIE

"Did something happen between you and Shepherd?" Tiffany asks as we check over each other's work. We have our first poetry project due, which needs to be flawless. This one assignment counts for about 20 percent of our final grade.

"No, why?"

She shrugs. "I don't know. It seems like he doesn't like you."

Shepherd has been making it clear how much he *doesn't like* me lately. He *doesn't like* me hanging around his friend. He *doesn't like* that I've become Mrs. Walker's favorite student in history class, so he undermines every positive comment she gives me by either deflecting with some crass joke or asking some idiotic question to make everyone laugh. He *doesn't like* that other people compliment me, so he tries avoiding spaces where we could end up near each other.

He *doesn't like* that I even breathe.

So I ignore and avoid him.

I'm about to tell Tiffany I don't care how Shepherd feels about me, but Jones pulls up. We jump down from the wall near the parking lot entrance and get into his car.

It's become a ritual on Wednesdays for the three of us to eat lunch together off campus, and I enjoy it. Jones always pays for us because chivalry isn't dead. Every time we offer to pay, he acts like we've killed his cat.

I'm comfortable with Jones. He reminds me of the brother I don't have. People think we're together, but we're not. I don't have those kinds of feelings for him, and he knows that. There's no doubt in my mind that he'd like something to happen between us, but I told him I didn't see him in that light.

Jones has also been telling people to book their tutoring sessions with me. Because of him, other people have come up to me asking for my availability. I don't need the money, but I'm happy to help.

"Where are we eating today?" Tiffany asks as we leave campus.

"How about the new place that opened up last weekend?" Jones suggests.

I have no idea about the new restaurant, so I ask about it.

"Sakura! Yeah, I'd be down to try it out," Tiffany exclaims.

"What kind of stuff is on their menu?" It sounds Japanese, and my relationship with sushi is ... well, complicated.

"Sushi, sashimi, you know, the usual Japanese food, soup," Tiffany says.

"I'm not a big fan of sushi. I'll pass."

"What?" Jones swivels his head around and looks at me while we're stopped at a red light.

"Pay attention to the road!" I say.

"We're not even moving," he says, indicating the red light. "Evie, have you tried it before?"

"What kind of question is that? Of course I've tried it."

"Maybe you tried some nasty ass sushi then 'cause the stuff is delicious."

We start moving again, and he turns to face the road ahead. Relieved, I let the conversation hang. I'm outvoted three to two. I resign myself to eating whatever other options are on the menu.

Sakura is a small, stylish Japanese restaurant seven minutes from campus. Our school gives us an hour for lunch. Couple that with the time we get between classes, and we're left with a good chunk of time to eat our food.

Jones and Tiffany already know what they're getting. I make the ordering process much faster because I decide on the most basic item on the menu.

"I'm good with the salad," I say to the waiter.

"Salad?" Tiffany and Jones both look at me, eyebrows raised.

"I told y'all I don't eat sushi."

"I'll have two California rolls instead of one, please," Jones says.

I look over at him. "Did you order that for you and your second gut? Because I'm not eating it."

Tiffany orders her roll and tells me I can order a veggie roll instead of the salad. I look at the veggie roll and decide it's just rice wrapped around a salad.

I pass.

We eat lunch and banter back and forth. Jones tries to get me to try his lunch, and I have to block his hands when he attempts to put a piece on my plate. I don't know how he does it. One minute I'm blocking his hands, and the next, my plate has three pieces of California roll on it. I get tunnel vision and focus solely on my salad at this point.

"You coming to my game tomorrow night?" Jones asks.

Tiffany answers with an affirmative while I chew my food. I haven't been to any of Paramount's football games. I'm usually either with my parents or doing something to destress from the week. I'm not a huge football fan so missing the games didn't faze me. This is the first time Jones has mentioned it, though.

"Why this game?" I ask, putting my fork down.

"Bruh, it's our homecoming game, and I've never seen you at *any* of the games. You don't like football?"

"It's not that I don't like football," I say. "But I'll be there since you're asking us to come."

On our way back to campus, Jones asks who I'm going to homecoming with. I have no plans to go to homecoming, which I've already told Tiffany. All her persuading didn't change my mind, and I doubt Jones's will either.

After the ride back to campus, with Jones and Tiffany tag-teaming to convince me of all the reasons I'm missing out on the full high school experience, I cave.

I freaking *cave.*

I'm so shocked when I hear myself say, "Alright," that I sit stupefied for a few seconds.

"That's what's up!" Jones says, grinning over at me as he puts the car in park. He closes the top of his Porsche, and we all get out. "So you going with me?"

"Yeah, sure. It's not a date, though, because I'm *not* ready for that level of attention. Especially not from the girls crushing on you or your friend who can't stand me."

Jones knows where we stand and agrees, "Who Shepherd? Nah, he doesn't know you. You straight. No worries."

"OK, Jones," Tiffany says, and I don't like how she says it.

"No, he's right. We're friends."

I don't see him in any other light.

I don't know much about football.

I know even less about what each player does. But when I'm around all these people, it's like I've taken on a whole new persona.

I cheer for PSA, screaming when our team makes a touchdown.

"P-S-A! P-S-A! Go Eagles! Whoooooo!"

Tiffany nudges me. "If I knew you would be this fun at games, I would have dragged you here ages ago!"

"What was that!" It's so loud I can barely hear her over everyone else's screams.

"You should've come to all the games!"

I grin back at her and nod. I may actually do that from now on.

Our team rips into Maverick, the other team playing tonight. I can make out a few golden PSA jerseys. Jones is number 24. I watch him on the field, standing behind the quarterback, Dudley, number 15.

When gameplay begins, I'm so impressed by Jones and every one of our players that I look at Tiffany in awe.

"I know! He's so freaking good!"

"Who!" We're still yelling because otherwise, it's impossible to hear.

"Shepherd! He's number 18! One of the wide receivers!"

I search the field and find the PSA number 18 jersey.

Shepherd flies from one end of the field to the other, maneuvering through several players.

He has skills.

Too bad he's an asshole.

About an hour later, the game ends, and we head down the bleachers to get to Jones before he returns to the locker room.

"How'd we do?" Jones asks, cheesing, a dimple forming in his cheek as he winks at us.

"You know you guys were freaking awesome!" Tiffany says.

I notice Tiffany glancing over at the other players as they leave the field. My curiosity piqued, I check out what has her so distracted.

When I look, I spot Shepherd taking off his helmet and heading toward someone in the crowd. I recognize the woman as soon as I see her. It's his mom, Jackie, whom I'd met a few weeks back when they came to our house. There's a man next to Jackie, but Shepherd is holding the helmet over his right shoulder, so I can't see the guy's face. I assume it's his dad.

Shepherd brings the helmet down from his shoulder.

My eyes flutter, and I narrow them, zeroing in on the man's face. Something's familiar about his face.

Within seconds, I have vivid flashbacks, a montage of images from the past playing across my mind.

Ethan.

Everything goes eerily still, and I'm eight years old again. I'm in a courtroom, and they're announcing that my brother's murderer gets to go free.

. . .

The drunk driver's family sits composed, almost unaffected by the proceedings. There's a boy, a curly-haired blond kid, and a thin woman seated beside him.

"Well, Mr. Buchanan." The judge draws my attention back to the man who killed my brother. "You have been acquitted of all charges. You are free to go."

"What? No!" I yell. My mother grabs me around the waist, thwarting my attempt to rush over to the guy.

Dad looks despondent.

I want to scream at him to do something. Anything. There is no way they are letting that criminal go.

No way.

I glare over at the kid when laughter erupts from that direction of the courtroom.

I immediately stiffen.

The smirk on his face as he stares over at me, and my parents, is forever etched in my memory. He doesn't give a damn that my brother is dead. His murderer of a dad is free to live out his life, while my twin is robbed of his at only eight.

No one cares.

Not the courts, not the cops, and certainly not the man who's responsible for taking my brother's life.

I stop breathing.

I'd recognize that man anywhere, the brown hair, the arrogant stance, the immaculate suit that screams wealth and entitlement.

Tiffany eventually nudges me. I blink my eyes, taking a deep, shaky breath.

"Evie ... are you—are you crying? What's wrong?"

I reach my hand up to touch my face and feel wetness

there. "I—uh," I attempt, my voice weak and my throat thick. "I need to get out of here."

I turn around and race to one of the exits. My vision blurs and I finally let the tears pour out.

Tiffany doesn't speak, but when she's had enough of my silence, she grabs my arm and steps out in front of me. "Evie, please tell me what's the matter," she says, distressed. "Why are you crying?"

I cover my face with my hands, shaking my head. "The guy in the suit that Shepherd was talking to. Is that his dad?" I ask, my voice broken.

"Y-yeah," Tiffany answers, hesitant. "Why?"

Fate has a twisted sense of humor.

The odds that I'd end up moving to the very town my brother's murderer lives in couldn't have been that high. Then to end up attending the same school as his son and to have had that son in my *house*.

These are the cards I've been dealt.

To think I've been dealing with the asshole offspring of the man who killed my brother and got away with it ...

The laughter starts from the bottom of my stomach and bubbles up into hysteria. I'm laughing so hard that a few seconds in, Tiffany starts laughing too.

"OK, good. You're OK. Don't do that again. It freaked me out. What the heck was all that about?"

"Bad memory. Could you take me home? I don't think I'm up for tonight." I said I would go with her to the after-game party one of the football players is throwing, but I can't.

"Evieeee," Tiffany whines.

"Homecoming is tomorrow. It's all the party I need for one week."

She rolls her eyes and then nods. "Fine, whatever."

No, not fine.

Nothing would ever go back to being *fine*, at least not for me.

A small part of me died in the courtroom that day.

Ethan.

The painful memory of that night he left us slashes through my soul.

If I'd known that night was the last one I would've had with my brother, the last words I'd say to him, I would've taken those hateful words back. I would've eaten sushi with him every day if it meant I could have him back.

But I wasn't that lucky.

Fate had other plans.

Chapter Eight

EVIE

"Honey, you look beautiful." Mom fastens the back of my dress, giving me a once-over before leaving me in front of her large bedroom mirror.

I check my reflection, smiling at what I see. The smile doesn't reach my eyes.

I'm draped in a satin dress, which extends to a little above my knees. Medium-sized pearls detail the thin line of the straps, and small slits go up to mid-thigh on either side. My twists hang over one shoulder.

I bend forward as Mom returns to secure a teardrop diamond necklace around my neck. I snap in the matching earrings. She attaches a red rose and pearl corsage around my wrist, a gift from Jones.

When Jones arrives fifteen minutes later, he steps out of his convertible and walks over to us, every bit the gentleman. He hands me a single red rose. "Good evening Mr. Richards, Mrs. Richards."

My parents exchange glances, impressed by the show.

"Jones, what are you doing?" I whisper, pulling him to my side.

"What? A guy can't bring his friend flowers?"

I smile, shaking my head.

"You look gorgeous, Evie."

"Thank you. The tux looks good on you." The white of my dress complements his black tuxedo.

My mother gets into photographer mode, snapping several photos of us, while Dad hangs back.

Afterward, Mom helps me with last-minute fixes here and there, and Dad talks to Jones. I don't catch much of what they're saying.

"Make sure you bring her home at an appropriate hour," Dad says.

"And in one piece," Mom adds.

And just like that, Jones and I leave for the homecoming dance.

I try not to think about yesterday. I didn't tell my parents I'd discovered who Shepherd was. I don't want to trigger any unpleasant memories for them. Telling them wouldn't bring Ethan back. I'm hoping tonight will keep me distracted.

When we get to the dance, I'm surprised to find that there's already a crowd of PSA students here. We're actually on time, so I'm amazed the place is already packed. Don't people usually arrive fashionably late for these things?

I get a text from Tiffany, assuring me she'll be here soon. I breathe a sigh of relief because apart from her, Jones, and Casey, I don't know or speak to many other people.

Jones and I go over to the refreshment tables and grab some finger food. A few of his friends come over, and they're not standing here for long before I can feel their eyes on me.

"You look great, Evie." This comes from one of his teammates.

I utter a word of thanks before bringing my eyes back to the fruit on my plate. We stand here like this for the next fifteen minutes, me in a group of Jones and his guy friends. It gets a little awkward. Jones realizes this and ushers me onto the dance floor.

I love dancing. I vibe to the music and let myself enjoy being led around and through the crowd. The song changes and we're still dancing, sometimes with the other people nearby.

Jones moves behind me, sliding his hands to my hips. Since we're dancing, I don't think much of it, and when he bends his head down to the crook of my neck, I still don't comment. But when he turns his face into my neck, I immediately turn to ask him what he's doing. His lips come close to mine, and I have to tilt my head away to create some space.

"Jones?"

He sighs.

OK. We need a break.

"I need to use the restroom." I quickly slip out of his grasp.

Where the heck is Tiffany?

As soon as I step foot into the restroom, I whip out my phone and send her a text.

A few seconds go by and she replies.

Tiffany: Casey and I are parking. Sorry.

Finally.

I exit the restroom and head down the long corridor

back to the main hall. Someone emerges from a side hall-way, blocking my path. I almost bump into him, but my clutch falls instead. I stoop to pick it up.

He doesn't move.

My eyes shift to immaculate dress shoes. They glide the rest of the way up to well-tailored black pants and a white button-down and tie.

My gaze lands on the last person I want to see tonight. Shepherd.

His face is drawn in an expression I can't read.

I groan.

Why now?

"Good evening, Evelyn." His voice is low, sounding almost pleasant.

Almost.

Surprised, I frown. This is the first time I've actually heard him say my name without his usual mocking tone.

I attempt to get around him.

He blocks me.

I look up at him, confused. "Is there a problem here?"

"I don't know, Evelyn, you tell me."

OK, what the hell is this about? What game is he playing now?

A few other people come down the corridor. I'm grateful because I don't care to deal with Shepherd right now, or any time for that matter.

When they get near us, he steps out of the way, and I use it as an opportunity to try and get by him again.

He bumps my shoulder and I swear he calls me out of my name, but there's no way he could have done that. I whirl around to face him, his back now to me.

"What did you call me?"

He turns to face me. "You heard me," he replies, smirking as he stares down at me through darkened blue eyes. I don't miss the way they roam over my body.

I'm reminded of the night of my dad's dinner, and all the times since then that he's disrespected me. An image of the arrogant kid in the courtroom those years ago, laughing at me while I sat grief-stricken, interposes itself. Before I can stop myself, I reach my free hand up and bring it across his face.

One of the girls exiting the restroom gasps, looking over at us as she and her friends gingerly walk by.

I'm about to turn and walk away when I hear a low chuckle. My mouth falls open in response, and he starts laughing at me.

A red fury rises inside me.

I start picturing him, and his dad, walking out of the courtroom that day, while my brother lay dead. My hand swings up as a reflex and I hit him across the face again. I come away with skin this time. There's a small scratch underneath his eye, and his face reddens where I hit him.

He stops laughing then, and his next movements are so sudden I barely register them.

Shepherd reaches out, grabbing me around my upper arms and roughly placing my back against the wall. He lowers his face and completely fills my vision, his nose inches from mine. Our eyes lock, his gaze intense, searching mine.

A muscle twitches in his top lip as he snarls at me. His eyes darken, blazing with anger, and something else I can't place.

No one has ever looked at me with such malice.

"You don't scare me." I curse the slight unsteadiness in my voice.

He brings his face even closer, and I swear I can smell the scent of his aftershave.

"Let ... go of me," I breathe out, aware of the picture we must be painting in this position.

"What if I don't want to, *E-vie*?" His lips part. I don't miss the way he calls me Evie, dragging out the syllables, mocking me again. "Aw. Are you gonna get Jones to beat me up?" he asks, sarcasm dripping from each word.

I furrow my brows in confusion. Why does he think Jones would need to fight for me? I am more than capable of doing that myself.

"Why would Jones lower himself to fight someone like you?" I ask. Shepherd outweighs me in physical strength but I know words. I'm good with words.

"Someone like me?" His expression falters, then his gaze narrows.

"You actually *enjoy* trying to make other people miserable. Jones doesn't. You're just a weak-minded tool whose parents don't love him enough so he—"

I don't finish because Shepherd's lips come crashing down on mine.

He crushes my mouth under the weight of his, and the insides of my upper lip grind against my teeth.

Reaching my palms up between us, I push hard at his chest, trying to turn my head away. He releases my arms only to hold my head in place, making it impossible. I open my mouth to bite down on his bottom lip, but he thrusts his tongue into my mouth. So I bite that instead, hard.

That gets him to release me. He touches a hand to his mouth, nostrils flaring, a wild look on his face.

"You're disgusting." I wipe my mouth with the back of my hand, meeting his gaze. "Don't you *ever* do that again, or I promise you'll regret it."

I don't give him a chance to respond. I shove at his chest, pick up my clutch from where it fell when he manhandled me, and stalk toward the main hall.

I recognize one of his friends standing at the edge of the hallway. But I ignore him, quickening my pace to get out of there.

SHEPHERD

Damn it!

I kissed Evelyn.

I freaking kissed her.

I don't know what the hell came over me. Call me a glutton for punishment, but I loved pissing her off. That final look she gave me before she stormed off ...

Yeah, we're not finished. Not by a long shot.

"Dude. What the hell was that?" Lucas asks, shaking his head.

"What?" I try to nurse my bruised tongue back to health by sucking on it.

"Shep, why'd you kiss Evie? Do you like her? 'Cause she's with Jones," he states.

I have a mind to tell him I don't give a damn who she's with but think better of it. The last thing I need is to give Lucas more ammo in his belief that I have a thing for her.

"She slapped me. Twice," I mumble. A few other people saw what happened in the hallway and were probably talking about it.

Good.

Jones is bound to find out before the night is out, and I'm in the mood to throw a few good punches right about now.

She *isn't* his girlfriend. Yet he acts like he owns her. He has some plan to go someplace with her tonight after the homecoming afterparty.

Not happening.

I've had my eye on Evelyn since she arrived on Jones's arm tonight.

She looks great, I won't deny that. But I'm not one of the groupies secretly pining for her like those guys were when she came in with Jones. When he danced with her, they all kept staring, watching the slits at the sides of her dress reveal way more leg than necessary. I swear they just want to sleep with her.

Jones is a part of that category, dancing on her, touching her.

When he tried kissing her, my chest felt weird. I had to look away, my hands fisting shut in my pockets.

There's something about all these guys lusting after her that I don't particularly like. Hell if I know why that is.

"Shep, don't do stuff like that. You don't want problems with Jones," Lucas says.

"Maybe I do," I counter.

Lucas narrows his eyes at me, confused. "Dude, you wanna tell me what is going on right now? Because I'm lost."

"I'll pass."

I walk ahead of him, and when we get back into the banquet hall, I immediately spot Chase.

She's with a group of people. She turns to me when I get to her, and a frown furrows her brow as she scrutinizes my face.

"What happened?" she asks.

I wince when she touches a sore spot near my eye.

"Ran into a cat," I deadpan.

Disregarding the others, I turn her around and place my hands on her hips, bringing my head down to her neck. I kiss her there, and of course she lets me.

She doesn't find me disgusting.

Chapter Nine

Shepherd hasn't changed.

He's the same arrogant kid who laughed at us in that courtroom. His dad probably hasn't changed either. They're both part of the same twisted tree. His father only hides it better.

A flash of the letter I wrote for my brother soon after the trial, comes to me.

I'll make them care, Ethan.
One day, when I'm all grown up,
I'm gonna make them hurt just as much as they hurt you.
Your twin,
Evie

I still owe it to him to make good on that promise. Fate has practically wrapped up this opportunity and handed it to me. And as the saying goes, I don't want to tempt her, so I'll accept it.

I have a mission to see that people pay for the crimes they committed, no matter how late the retribution may be.

I change out of my homecoming dress and put on the full cloak of reckoning that fate and time have afforded me.

My booted stilettos make noises against the cobblestones as Tiffany and I walk up the path to the afterparty.

"Oh my gosh! Evie, look!" Tiffany runs over to the photo booth. "Come on! We have to get one."

From the different props provided, I take the devil's horns and pitchfork, and she puts on angel wings and a halo. We snap several silly Polaroids, then head through the glass doors of the venue.

The lighting in the huge room makes it difficult to make out faces, unless we're in reasonable distance of them.

The place is set up like a lounge. We text Jones, letting him know we're here so he can come get us.

"Damn, Evie. You look good!" he says when he reaches us. "As do you, Tiffany."

"I like your entire vibe," Tiffany offers, complimenting him in return. Jones is wearing a navy button-down that accentuates his muscles.

"We're back there." We follow him to the other side of the room. "Blame" by Calvin Harris blares in the background. There are a few people dancing, while others are in conversation.

We get to the back of the room, and I tamp down on my immediate animosity when I notice Shepherd amid the crowd. I remind myself that I need to start stifling my aversion to him so I can have the desired outcome I want later.

I somehow end up standing near him. Believing I can actually do this, I grin and bear it.

"I thought you found me disgusting," he says after a while. "How come you're not moving away from me?"

I know he's looking for a rise out of me. He couldn't retaliate by hitting me when I'd slapped him earlier so he's choosing to punish me by some other means. I won't delude myself into thinking Shepherd actually *wanted* to kiss me.

I guess he isn't the type to hit women. Did his dad sneak that lesson in there by some miracle? The other ones seem to have evaded both father and son.

Jackie's likely the only form of light in the darkness of that house. Come to think of it, I don't remember seeing her at the courthouse that day.

Strange.

"Thought you hated me," Shepherd continues. "Especially after what happened earlier."

"Enemies closer and all that," I conclude for him.

He laughs. And though it doesn't seem like he's trying to tease or upset me, every time he's done this it's been to annoy me.

I don't take the bait.

I walk away from him instead, following Tiffany, Jones, and a few others onto the dance floor.

Two things happen while we're dancing.

First, Jones is clingy, warding off the guys who try to dance with me for longer than *he* wants.

Not cool.

And second, one of those guys is Shepherd.

I can't fathom Shepherd's reason for wanting to dance with me. He's made his aversion to me obvious in every and all situations. I startle when he places his hand on my waist, turning me to face him.

I try not to react when I meet his gaze, glancing away from him and using the music as a distraction.

At one point, he slides his palms to the tops of my hips, where the black crop top I'm wearing leaves my skin bare.

I meet his gaze.

Then I have the oddest reaction. My stomach gets knotted, and there's this pooling sensation where he's holding me. It's like I want him to ... to ... I don't know, squeeze me there or something. Freaked out by it, I step out of his embrace.

Jones chooses that very moment to come over to us.

Grateful, I heave an inward sigh and for the next hour I'm whirling around, dancing from partner to partner. I dance with Tiffany and a group of girls at one point, but I don't dare dance with Shepherd again.

I can't.

When we're getting ready to leave, Casey asks to ride with Tiffany. She of course says yes.

I'm heading out with them, when Jones catches up to us and grabs my arm.

"Hey, wanna ride with me? Give Casey and Tiffany some privacy." He shifts his gaze between the two, trying to clue me in.

Tiffany and Casey?

I couldn't have been that blind. She never said anything about being into him.

"It's not like that with them," I explain, because Jones must be mistaken.

"It's like that for him."

Um, excuse me. I mean, they were each other's date for homecoming. But that happened by default since Casey didn't have anyone to go with, and neither did she.

I let Tiffany know the change, and she and Casey head out.

I'm about to get into Jones's car when a hand slides over mine and tugs me back.

I jerk my head around to find Shepherd standing behind me.

"What're you doing? Let go of my hand." I tug at my hand.

"Shep, what's going on?" Jones comes over to our side of the car.

"I'm not letting you do it." His grip tightens, and as his words register, I pause my attempts at pulling free.

"The hell are you talking about, bro?" Jones asks.

The two of them stare at each other and when my patience all but vanishes I ask, "Do what?" My hand still held prisoner, I turn to Shepherd. "Will you let go? It hurts."

He instantly opens his palm and lifts my hand up, inspecting it before releasing me.

"Why don't you go back in there and get Chase? 'Cause something's up with you, man." Jones reaches for my hand.

I pull it behind me, backing up slightly. Neither has yet to explain what Shepherd meant by not *letting* Jones *do it*.

"I'm not going anywhere with anyone until someone explains what's going on."

Jones lets out a frustrated sigh and shakes his head. "Evie, come on, let's go. I just wanna show you a good time."

"If a *good time* means taking her anywhere but home, I don't think her *dad* would appreciate that." Shepherd glares at him.

"Yo, you never even met her dad, so shut the hell up."

"I've met *and* had conversations with Evelyn's dad, but that's beside the damned point. I'm not letting you take her anywhere tonight."

I call Tiffany, because I'm not even sure what to think of all this.

Jones was trying to take me somewhere? What, did he think he could persuade me to be with him?

He's been acting weird all night, but I would never have thought him capable of something like this.

Tiffany doesn't answer, so I keep calling her. I don't want to bother my parents. It's after midnight, and I told them not to wait up. I'm supposed to be back before one though, so I only have within the hour to get home.

I whirl around when Jones lunges at Shepherd, punching him across the face. The two of them start fighting, and when I yell at them to stop, they keep going at it.

I run back inside and try to get help.

Lucas and Dudley come with a few other guys, and some girls follow.

Two guys hold on to Shepherd. The others restrain Jones, dragging them apart.

SHEPHERD

It was only a matter of damned time.

I knew tonight would end up like this.

Jones has been pissing me off all night with his constant display over Evelyn. He kept interrupting the guys whenever they danced with her, cutting in as if she came here just for him.

She didn't.

I swear he only wanted to make sure that by the end of the night, she left with him.

I got a good read on Evelyn tonight, and she isn't easy like some of the girls he's grown accustomed to. I'm pretty sure she wouldn't go anywhere with him that involved a bed and their two bodies slapping together.

That image alone makes my stomach churn.

"What the hell, Shep? What's your problem?" Jones yells, John and another teammate struggling to hold him back.

"You punched me first!" I shout. Dudley and Lucas loosen their grip on me.

"What does what I do with Evie have to do with you?"

"Nothing. I don't like to see girls taken advantage of."

"Bullshit, Shepherd! What do you call the motto you live by every damned day? Every girl you're with is the epitome of you *taking advantage*. You cycle through chicks like girls change their underwear, so don't give me that shit."

"Oh yeah! Well at least they *know* where they stand, and still want to be with me."

"Watch out, bro. Your mommy issues are startin' to show."

Beanca steps in. "Shut the hell up, Jones. Don't bring family into this."

I'm straining at the guys to let me go so I can mess him up. Two more of my teammates come against me, making it impossible for me to free myself.

"Tell Shep to stop butting into my shit!"

"He's pissed his well-laid plans to get *laid* tonight didn't work out."

"Hey, yo, shut the hell up!"

"Alright how about the *both* of you shut up! Shepherd, let's go." Beanca gestures at the guys to let me go, then grabs a hold of my arm.

I look over at Evelyn and she has her phone to her ear, probably calling someone to come get her.

Good.

Anyone but Jones.

Chase reaches us and instantly starts worrying over me. Beanca dabs at the corner of my cut lip.

My gaze shifts from them and back over to Evelyn. She takes the phone from her ear and goes over to talk to Jones.

I can't make out what they're saying from where I'm standing, but there's no way she'll leave with him. Not after what happened.

She touches a bruise on his face, and I look down at my reddened knuckles.

Chase pulls a piece of tissue from her purse and holds it against my hand. I look up to find Evelyn inspecting Jones's bruises.

A muscle in my jaw twitches.

I fight this intense need to go over there and drag her the hell away from him.

I don't expect her to make him public enemy number one, but caring for him after what he was planning to do …

I brush Chase's hand away and rake my bruised hand roughly through my hair. I wince from the movement, but welcome the pain.

"I'm good," I say to Beanca when she tries grabbing hold of my hand.

"Shep, why'd you pick a fight with him?" Chase asks.

I don't answer. Again my eyes wander over to where Jones and Evelyn are standing.

She's opening the passenger side door.

My fists clench.

Don't.

She reaches into the back of the car, and I relax when she pulls out what looks like a sweater and a couple of books. She says something else to him.

Jones turns away from her, gets in his car, and drives off, leaving her standing there.

Evelyn looks down at her phone.

"Shep, let's go," Chase says, pulling on my arm as the group disbands, some people heading to their cars.

I don't budge. "You guys go ahead."

Lucas side-eyes me, frowning, before going back inside with his date and a few others.

"Bee, can Chase ride with you?"

"Why?" she asks, looking beyond me and over at Evelyn. "Why can't *you* take Chase home? She came with you."

"Because I can't let Evelyn stand out here alone this late waiting on a ride." I state the obvious. "Look, I don't know how long she needs to wait out here, and Chase isn't all that patient so will you take her?"

"Yeah, I'm with Shep on this," Chase adds. "I'm gonna need that ride. I don't see the point in standing out here waiting on *her* to get a ride home." She points in Evelyn's direction.

"Whatever, just text me when you get home," Beanca says.

When they leave, I walk over to Evelyn.

She's browsing through social media and startles when I sidle up to her. I'm sure I'm the last person she expects to find standing here beside her.

"What are you doing?" she asks. "Don't you have some girl to go pass the time with?"

"Careful, *E-vie*, I might think you're jealous."

She scoffs, then proceeds to scroll through her phone.

I'm nosy, so I look.

"I'm sorry do you need something?" She doesn't bother looking at me.

I pull my cell phone from my pocket. "What's your username?" Of course I already know it, but she doesn't know that.

"Are you serious?"

"Yup."

She shows me her username and I follow her. She accepts my request but doesn't follow back.

I could comment on that, but the fact she even showed me the username was rare enough of an accomplishment.

"How're you getting home?" I ask.

"My dad."

"Are you OK?"

"Nope."

"I'm sorry for how I acted earlier tonight." Her fingers freeze on her phone screen. "I know what I said upset you. It was rude. And how I treated you was ... I'm sorry."

I'm not the apologetic type. So when the words leave my mouth, even I'm trying to come to terms with what I've said. But I regret how I behaved with her, the things I said, what I did.

She's silent for a second and then says, "That's OK. Some people can't help where they come from. The apple doesn't fall far from the tree and all that."

"Don't do that. Don't talk like you know anything about me, Evelyn."

She turns to face me then, her eyes staring daggers into mine.

"Shepherd, I'm sorry," she says, schooling her features.

Something inside me jolts when she says my name.

I'm curious about what she wanted to say. There was passion behind those brown eyes, before she concealed it.

"And since I owe you one for helping me out tonight, how about I help you out in history?"

I'm so thrown off, I don't know what to say. "What?"

Evelyn *willingly* being nice to me feels too good to be true.

"If you don't want my help, then fine, forget I even—"

"No. I mean, yeah. I'd love it if you could help me out," I say, interrupting her. The last thing I want is for her to renege.

"Good."

We talk about it a little and figure out a schedule, and before I know it, her dad's pulling up.

"Is your place good?" she asks.

"I thought we'd do it at school or something."

"I'm not waiting behind after school for you to finish practice. That's like two hours long. Text me your address and I'll come." She gives me her number; then we walk over to her dad's truck.

"Good evening, Shepherd, how's it going?" her dad asks.

"Doing pretty good, sir. And you?"

"Can't complain."

Evelyn gets in.

"Well, I hope you get home safe, young man."

They leave and I'm feeling good, like I hung the moon or some shit.

If anyone had told me that by the end of the night I would:

A. have Evelyn not hate me,

B. have her give me her number, or

C. have plans for her to come over to my place, I would have said they were batshit crazy with either one of those options.

Having all three happen in one night, I'm speechless.

Chapter Ten

EVIE

"You're gonna be doing what!" Tiffany's brows climb so high they almost disappear into her hairline.

"Tutoring Shepherd."

It can't be more perfect. Our sessions will allow me into Shepherd's inner sanctum, a gateway to Mr. Michael Buchanan, his father.

What happened this past weekend was a clear sign that Shepherd didn't dislike me. If he did, he would've let Jones use me.

So I have an angle.

I have a path.

And this time Mr. Buchanan and his son won't have a damned thing to laugh about.

"Are you serious? He asked you to tutor him?"

"Nope. I offered."

"What? I thought you two didn't even like each other."

"Correction. If anything, he's the one who had a

problem with me. Anyway, after what happened with Jones, he kind of went up a few notches."

"Evie, even I could've told you that guys like Jones don't hang around you because you're like a *sister* to them." Tiffany rolls her eyes, using air quotes to emphasize 'sister.'

"You might've thought so, but I even hinted that he wanted more."

"Yeah, well, Jones and I are on a break. And it's not like he actually did anything. I wouldn't have slept with him, and he wouldn't have forced me to. So, it would've ended up like this either way."

"When do you think we'll start hanging out again? With Jones, I mean. I actually looked forward to our lunches."

"Whenever he's ready. After I told him we should pause our sessions for a little bit, he got upset. I took my stuff out of his car. You should have seen us. It was so petty, especially when he drove off and left me there. He reminds me so much of Ethan, it's crazy."

"Ethan? Who's that?"

I freeze.

I've never mentioned my brother to anyone, not even Tiffany. It's not like I tried keeping it a secret that I had a twin brother who was killed. It just never came up in conversation.

"Ethan is—was, my brother. My twin. He got killed in a car accident when we were little."

"Wow, Evie. I'm so sorry. If you don't want to talk about it, you don't have to."

"No, I'm OK."

"Sooo, what caused the accident?" Tiffany asks, hesitant.

"We were on our way home from dinner and some guy swerved into us from the left lane. My dad was ... distracted.

By the time he saw what was happening, our car spun into the guardrail of the embankment. The part of the van where my brother was sitting took the brunt of the hit. He died at the scene."

When I finish telling her the rest of what happened, leaving names out, she's indignant.

"That's messed up! How did he get away with killing someone when alcohol was involved?"

I shrug. "Money. Connections. The usual."

She doesn't know what to say.

"I looked into the case," I continue. "A normal person would've gone to prison for at least three years, but they let him off. They didn't care about my brother, and that's why they have to pay."

"What do you mean?" She frowns, and I realize I've said my thoughts aloud.

"You know, karma and stuff. I don't think his murderer will be able to escape that." I smile at her and then add, "I hear she can be a bitch." We're both laughing as we enter third period.

Elliot comes up to me with the results of our test from last Friday. He's one of the guys I've been tutoring after school.

"You're awesome! Look at this." His paper has a very vivid B+ written in the top right corner. It's not an A, but for Elliot it may as well be. He's been pulling a D-average in our class. He only needed better strategies for studying and managing his time.

"That's all you, Elliot. Nice!"

He holds a hand up for a high-five, and I'm about to oblige, when Shepherd's hand connects with his before I get the chance.

"What's up, Shep? I didn't see you come in, man," Elliot says, turning to Shepherd.

Shepherd squeezes himself between Tiffany and me, separating us.

"Hey, Shep," Tiffany says.

I move away, creating some distance between us.

Shepherd nods at them, then faces me. "Hey, am I gonna see you later?"

The way he says it makes it sound more intimate than necessary. Tiffany's gaze instantly shifts to me.

"For tutoring? Yeah, I'll be there."

"Evie, I was wondering"—Elliot ushers me off to a side of the room where we can speak privately—"is there any way you could do me a solid and—"

He doesn't get to finish, because Shepherd interrupts, shuffling himself between us. He places an arm over Elliot's shoulder. "What's the secret?" he whispers in Elliot's direction.

I pause, narrowing my eyes in confusion.

What was Shepherd's problem? I thought we'd come to some level of truce. Maybe that was wishful thinking.

"Shepherd," I say.

He brings his attention to me. Something strange passes between us, but I can't decipher what it is.

"What are you doing?" I ask.

His gaze flickers to my mouth and then back up to my eyes. He straightens and removes his arm from Elliot. "Nothing. Sorry about that." He turns and heads to his seat, leaving me standing there with Elliot.

"Go ahead," I say woodenly.

Elliot ruffles his hair. "Do you write papers for people? Because I was wondering if you could write my essay." He quickly adds, "I can pay you for it, of course."

"No. I don't cheat. I just tutor."

"That's cool. I get it." He's about to step away but hesitates. "Oh by the way, I know you're into poetry so I was wanting to ask ... would you be interested in going to a poetry slam with me?"

My automatic answer would have been no, because I'm not interested in Elliot, but he's super sweet for paying attention to my interest in poetry. That changes the invitation in my eyes.

"Are you serious? Of course! When is it?"

He tells me some of the details and when Mrs. Walker arrives to start class, he promises to text me the rest.

SHEPHERD

I don't have anything against Elliot. Dude's a standup kid. I question my sanity when I wish he might just disappear.

I realize the absurdity of my thoughts and try to suppress my annoyance.

Frowning to myself, I shake my head. Finding no reason for my irritation, I attempt to focus on Walker's lecture. Only thing is, listening to her is like one of those episodes of *Charlie Brown*. I'm Charlie and she's one of the adults.

I get nothing.

I sneak my phone out and send a text to Evelyn.

Me: I'll be a little late today after practice. That OK?

It takes a little while for her to respond, but the three ellipses finally pop up and I wait.

Evelyn: Define 'a little.'

I chuckle to myself.

Me: Like ten/fifteen minutes.

I don't get a response for another few minutes.

Evelyn: Was that wait time OK *for you?*

At first I'm confused by her question. But when I register that she's referring to how long it took her to reply to my text, I start laughing.

I look up to find Walker and the rest of the class staring at me.

"Mr. Buchanan, would you mind telling me and the rest of class what so amuses you about the French and Indian War?"

I clear my throat and sit up a little straighter. "Nothing, ma'am. I apologize."

She pushes her glasses up the bridge of her nose and continues her lecture.

Me: Lol why do you have to be difficult?

Evelyn: Because it's you.

If this were any other girl, I'd assume she was flirting with me. But it's Evelyn, so I quickly ditch the idea.

Me: What's that supposed to mean?

Evelyn: Shepherd, pay attention.

It's the third time she's used my name, and even though it's in text, I don't know, it makes me feel all close to her or something.

Me: Yes ma'am.

I pocket my phone and attempt to refocus on the lecture.

A few hours later, I notice Evelyn's not in the cafeteria during lunch. Tiffany and Casey are here though. I'm curious, but I leave it there.

"Earth to Shep. Dude, where are you at?" Lucas asks, chewing on one of his chicken tenders. "Why're you so distracted lately?"

"Define distracted." I'm brought back to this morning's text conversation with Evelyn. A smile cracks my lips, and I look at my phone where I'm scrolling through her Our Social page.

"See, like that. What's got you cheesin' like that all the damned time?"

Was I cheesing?

I look at Lucas, stone-faced now. "So instead, I should be sulking at the bad shit in my life."

"Nah, dude, I wasn't saying that."

"I guess it's good you've found something that makes you smile like that, Shep," Beanca says, pushing the food around on her tray. "I haven't seen one of those on you in a while."

"*What* are you guys talking about? There's no special thing that's out here making me smile. Y'all are acting like I'm always moping around. Which is *the* furthest from the truth by the way. I'm having fun with Chase."

Beanca looks over at me like she doesn't buy what I'm saying, and Lucas picks up another chicken tender, biting into it.

"So, when do you and Jones plan to patch things up?" Beanca asks.

"I don't know, Bee. When he decides to get over himself, I guess."

"I still don't get why you two were fighting over her," she continues. "It's not like you like Evie, and it's not even like she and Jones are together."

"How do you know Shep doesn't like her?"

"Because he's with Chase, and Evelyn probably wouldn't even give him the time of day."

Lucas and Beanca continue bickering about my personal life as if I'm not sitting right across from them.

"She goes for guys like Jones," Beanca states.

"Whoa, that's so stereotypical of you, Bee. Just because

they're both Black, doesn't mean she would automatically cancel all other types of guys. Shep included."

"But you're assuming Shep's type of hot is what all girls like. Just because Chase, Lexie, and a bunch of other girls like him, doesn't *automatically* mean Evie would too. The fact that she hangs around Jones a lot, and even went to homecoming with him, tells me the kind of guys she's into."

I'm so over this conversation.

"I'm *not* interested in Evelyn, so this topic is pointless." I start getting up. "And by the way, Bee, I'm not *with* Chase. We have fun together from time to time. That's it."

Beanca's eyes meet mine and I notice a faint smile on her lips. "Well you should let Chase know. You know, in case she starts getting other ideas."

"Chase and I both know where we stand, but thanks for the warning." I leave the cafeteria and don't get but ten steps past the double doors before John walks up.

"Heads up. Practice got pushed back thirty minutes. Coach has some impromptu faculty meeting. He'll meet us in the locker rooms after."

Damn it.

I have a session with Evelyn planned for five. I already told her I'll be running late, but forty-five minutes is overkill. I don't want to cancel though, because I need the help.

"You think Coach'll be mad if I leave early?"

"All I know is, he didn't let Jones leave early when he'd asked. And he definitely got mad when Dudley had a family emergency that caused him to miss out that one time."

"Yeah but Dudley's the quarterback. Him missing practice is like playing football without the ball." I know I sound ridiculous, but I don't have many options here and I know it.

"OK, yeah, and you're a wide receiver."

He's got several points. I dread what I have to do, but it's the only option open to me.

During practice after school, when we're about an hour and a half in, I tell Coach I have to relieve myself. He looks aggravated but waves me off. I run to the locker room, and text Evelyn.

Me: Hey. Don't be pissed. I'm gonna be another thirty minutes.

When she doesn't answer right away, I get antsy. I don't have a lot of time to wait around for a response to my message.

Then I see that she's typing.

Evelyn: I'm on my way to your place now. Should I head back home then?

Me: No. I can't cancel. Look, if you get to my place and my dad's not there you can use the key. It's in the flower box on the right windowsill, near the flowers at the front edge.

Evelyn: OK cool.

I drop the phone back into my bag and close the locker before heading back out to the field.

Within the next thirty minutes practice ends and I tear off the field. I get out of the shower and am getting dressed, when Jones comes over to my locker.

"Bro, I owe you an apology," he says.

"Nah, you're good, man." I wasn't upset with Jones. We were all waiting for him to come around.

"I was talking to Evie today and she gave me my ass. Told me exactly how things would have gone down had I tried anything with her," he continues.

So that's where she was during lunch.

"Oh yeah?" I say, dragging on my shirt.

"Yeah, man. I'm relieved things are back to normal. I

hated the way I left things." He hooks an arm over my shoulder. "At first, I thought you did all that 'cause you were into her." He pauses, removes his arm, then straightens up. "I understand you wanted to help a brother out. Guess you did it for me to see the value in her. She's honestly the complete package. Good looking out." He holds his hand out for a fist bump, and we're cool again.

By the time I'm in my car and on my way home, the sky opens up and it's pouring.

Great.

I'm trying to get home as fast as I can, but there's traffic and the roads are wet.

I finally pull into my driveway, and it's over an hour after our scheduled time. I don't even bother opening up the garage, I park in the driveway and run to my front door, getting drenched on my way there.

As soon as I open up, I'm about to call for Evelyn, but I hear voices coming from my dad's office. Recognizing my dad's hostile voice, and Evelyn's quiet responses, I jog down that hallway.

"I shouldn't have come in here. I'm sorry," Evelyn says.

"I don't know why Shepherd would think it's OK for a perfect stranger to enter our house with none of us home. Do not step a foot back into this office unless you've been invited. Have I made myself clear?"

"Yes, Mr. Buchanan."

"What's going on?" I push at my dad's door, entering his office to find Evelyn standing in front of him with her hands clasped, as if she's some child being punished. I don't like the way my dad's looking at her, so I place my hand at her waist and hug her to my side.

"There you are," I say to her. "Why didn't you go up to my room to wait?"

She startles and looks up at me. Her brown eyes travel over my wet hair and soaked clothes. "I didn't know where your room was and even if I did I wouldn't have gone in there without you here."

"Well you sure as hell entered this room," my dad says, his eyes not wavering from her.

"You're so wet. Aren't you cold?" she asks, a frown creasing her brows. She brings her small hand to my neck, the back of it warm against my skin there.

I look down at her, my eyes traveling over her features, searching. For what? I don't know. Her touch feels natural, so unlike the hostility that's often been a given between us. I'm a bit taken aback by it.

"You should change out of those clothes," she says, before turning to my dad. "Again, I'm sorry, Mr. Buchanan. It won't happen again."

We leave his office, and my dad reiterates, "Shepherd, see to it that your friends know this room is off-limits. I don't want to have my office behind lock and key in my own house."

"I'm sorry about my dad." I'm embarrassed and don't know what else to say.

Evelyn grabs her backpack from the chair in the foyer and follows me. "It's fine. I was the one in the wrong. I wandered around and ended up in the wrong place. No worries."

We get to my room, and I pull off my T-shirt, opening a drawer to grab a change of clothes. I glance over at Evelyn to find her eyes on me.

Her gaze shifts to take in the rest of my room.

I've got a pretty good physique so when her gaze flutters back to my torso, I turn and stroll to the bathroom.

"I'll be right out," I say, smiling to myself.

I look myself over in the mirror and struggle to tame the wild mop of curls on my head after I towel it dry. I rake my fingers through it, trying to get the curls to sit right and when they don't, I get irritated.

"Forget it." I don't know why I care anyway.

I try fixing them again.

I return to the room and find Evelyn standing by one of the center windows.

My windows overlook a huge backyard that stretches into the woods behind our house. We live on about twenty acres of land, and our house is about a ten-minute drive to our neighbors on either side of us. It's a traditional home, large enough to fit five families.

I observe Evelyn in the backdrop of my bedroom. In my wildest dreams I could never have imagined her being in my house, let alone my room. My neck heats, and I'm anxious all of a sudden.

What the hell am I thinking?

I mentally shake myself and clear my throat.

She turns at the sound and glances over at me. She's so beautiful that all I can do is stare at her. She's in skinny jeans and a long-sleeved top but still manages to look this good.

"Ready?" She reaches for her bag, opens it, then sits Indian-style on the carpeted floor.

"Did you want anything to drink or eat? Considering you had to wait a while."

"No, I'm good. Let's start."

I grab my laptop, journal and history textbook and join her on the floor.

For the next hour, I try to concentrate on the material. Evelyn helps me with strategies for committing it to memory. When she speaks, at times I can't help staring at her. At her hair, at her eyes, at her mouth.

Her long twists fall down her shoulders whenever she leans forward to show me something. She constantly pushes them back up. The action exposes her neck to me. I don't know if it's because that's the only skin she's showing, but every time she does it, I find myself staring at the raised scar there.

"What?" she asks when she catches me staring.

"How'd you get that?" I point to the raised ridge, visible above the white neckline of her shirt.

"It's nothing. A battle scar from childhood. Why?"

"Nothing," I reply, refocusing my attention on what we're reviewing. If she doesn't want to explain further, I'm not going to pry.

When we finish, she texts her dad to come get her.

"Do you mind if we go out back?" she asks, rising from the carpet and walking over to the door. "It's nice out and the rain's eased up."

"Sure," I reply without hesitation. I lead us downstairs and to the back porch.

Once we're outside, it's a little chilly and there's still a drizzle. I head back inside, throw a jacket on and bring her another.

"Here." I place the jacket over her shoulders.

She accepts it, holding it by its lapels. "Thanks."

We stand in silence for a while.

"It's so beautiful here," she says.

I watch her; then I look out at the tall oak trees, their leaves dripping from the rain. "Yeah, I guess it is."

"Do you ever go camping?"

"Here?" I return my full attention to her. "No, but I have gone camping before."

"How come not here? You have a good setup." She gestures toward the forest lining our property.

"I guess it's not as exciting, since I'd still be at home, right?"

"You have a point. But, if I lived here, I'd still do it. At least once, anyway."

In all my years of living in this house, I've never once looked at my backyard in that fanciful light. I find myself at odds with her ability to see such positivity in a place where I'd been abandoned. I don't know what comes over me, but I lash out. "Yeah, well it's a good thing you don't live here then."

"That was rude," she states flatly.

"Just speaking the facts, babe."

"Don't call me babe," she snaps, handing me my jacket before reentering the house.

"And don't mistake my honesty for rudeness," I reply, following her.

She ignores me and runs upstairs to get her stuff. When she comes back down, I can tell she's upset with me, judging by the way she avoids looking in my direction. She strides to the front door. Before she can open it, I grab hold of her hand. She tries to pull free, but I tighten my grip.

"Let me go." She struggles to pull her hand from mine, giving up once she realizes the futility of her actions.

She still doesn't look at me.

I don't let her go.

She sighs heavily.

We stand like this for at least a minute, her refusing to face me and me still holding on to her hand.

I crack first.

"Evelyn, I'm sorry. I'm sorry if what I said upset you."

"Then why'd you say it?" She turns to face me.

"I don't know. I just ... I have a lot of memories—bad memories of stuff that happened when I was younger. I guess when you said what you said, it triggered me or something." I answer her truthfully, realizing how much I revealed to her about my childhood in this house.

"Shepherd," she says, regretful. "My bad. I didn't mean to. I—"

"Of course you didn't. You didn't know, couldn't know."

Her eyes meet mine.

I see the vulnerability there that I've only seen a glimpse of once before, and it makes me want to pull her into me.

Her cell phone goes off, interrupting the moment. That's when we realize I still have her hand in mine. I release her, and she reaches for the phone.

"Dad, I'm coming out," she says before hanging up. Then Evelyn does something completely unexpected. She reaches her arms around me and brings herself against me.

I'm stunned.

I stand there for a good couple of seconds before I return her embrace. She feels and smells so good. All too soon, she loosens her arms and we separate.

"See you tomorrow," she says.

I walk her out and wave to her dad before heading back inside.

I'm standing there like an idiot looking at the door when my dad says, "I know your game is scheduled for Thursday. Did Jackie let you know you have to stand in for me this Friday evening?"

"Yeah she told me."

Jackie has an upcoming showcase. It ended up in a schedule conflict with a weekend conference my dad needs to attend. He works in corporate sales. She's in finance and tech. Businesswise, they complement each other. I think that's the only reason they've lasted. My dad's never professed to be a loyal lover and never has been. He's had a lot of women. Jackie looks the other way at his indiscretions.

Like I said, their relationship is a business one. But hey, it works for them. I only wish she'd been one of the first women after my mom left.

"How's school?" he asks, breaking my train of thought.

I don't know if he's asking me because he cares or because he wants to verify I need a tutor.

Either way, I fill him in.

"As long as you do your share in this family."

By my share he means keeping the Buchanan name squeaky clean. No drugs, no DUIs, no failing grades, nothing that could affect our family's reputation in the community. My uncle is a local politician. So was their father before them.

We're all expected to toe the line.

"Yes, sir."

I head back up to my room to continue studying, and attempt to use at least one of the strategies I learned this evening.

Chapter Eleven

EVIE

Knowing Shepherd didn't have some grandiose childhood should make me happy. I should be jumping for joy that the Buchanan family had its own tragedies. But there was something about Shepherd's whole being that changed when he mentioned his past. I felt that part of him calling to some lost part of me.

Ethan.

This is about Ethan.

I need to remember why exactly I'm doing all this. I can't let Shepherd's comments about his past move me. If anything, it should strengthen my resolve since his dad has clearly messed up more than one life.

It's been a couple of weeks since I started tutoring him, and our sessions have gone pretty well. It's too soon to tell if he's internalized everything because we haven't had any exams recently. Outside of tutoring, we greet each other and have brief conversations here and there. We're civil, and that works fine for me, for now.

Mr. Buchanan isn't an easy read. What I thought would be a simple plan turns out to have more moveable parts to work around. I've been scoping out possible ways to plant my camera in his office, where he won't detect it. I've also figured out the perfect angle to film. That way the evidence won't be contested.

"I see two seats over there," Elliot says.

I follow him to sit in one of two available spots on a couch.

We're at a bookstore in a strip mall, where they're keeping the slam poetry event he'd told me about. Though small, it's set up almost like an amphitheater. The whole place has this cozy, dimly lit aesthetic. It isn't too crowded, the seating arrangement making it possible to gauge the audience's reaction to each poet. As each person goes up, they present either an original piece or recite one of their favorites. I also brought a piece to share.

"Thanks for inviting me," I say.

"For sure. I thought you'd like it."

After listening to a handful of people, I decide to get us some smoothies. I go to the café area, intending to buy them and return quickly. But I spot Chase and Shepherd eating together at a burger joint.

I pause mid-stride, observing the way they laugh with each other, Chase touching him playfully on his arm.

I ignore them, collecting the smoothies before making my way back. I chalk it up to wanting to give them their privacy. After all, I don't care who Shepherd's messing around with.

I'm about to turn the corner and walk the last few feet to the bookstore, when Shepherd stops me.

"Evelyn?" He takes hold of my upper arm and turns me to face him.

"What?"

He frowns. "What's wrong?"

"What do you mean? Nothing's wrong, Shepherd. I'm fine."

"If you were *fine*, then you wouldn't look upset. And you would've said something to me just now instead of walking away like you didn't know I was there. What did I do?"

"*Nothing*. Did you not just hear me tell you that I'm fine?" I shrug his hand from my arm. "You can go back to your girlfriend."

He's silent but continues watching me.

"She's not my girlfriend, Ev." He's never called me *Ev* before.

I look up at him, pursing my lips.

"She's not, OK," he repeats.

An odd sensation edges its way into my stomach.

He holds my hands in his, the cold smoothies between us. Warmth emanates from his palms where they cover me.

"What are you doing here with Elliot?" he asks.

"How—how do you know I'm with Elliot?"

He shrugs, "PSA. Word spreads."

"Then you should already *know* there's a poetry slam going on in the bookstore a few stores down from here." I avert my gaze, then ask, "What are you and Chase doing here?"

He hesitates, then rakes a hand through his hair. "We were watching a movie."

I nod. "Well, you guys have fun. I'll see you around." I try to turn and leave, but he stops me.

"Ev, wait. What do you think is going on between Chase and me?"

"It doesn't matter. And why do you keep calling me *Ev?*"

He narrows his gaze at me, then says, "Because it's short for Evelyn."

"Actually no, Evie is."

"So is Ev."

I roll my eyes. "I'm heading back. Elliot's probably wondering where I am."

I hurry back to the slam session.

When not even a half hour later, Chase and Shepherd enter the bookstore, I grind my teeth, refocusing my attention to the stage.

We listen to another piece and then the host invites me to go up.

"The next poet to grace us with an original piece is Evelyn Richards."

Elliot starts cheering, and a few others join him as I bring one of my poetry journals up to the stage with me. I've memorized the poem I want to recite but bring the journal in case I forget a line or something.

I approach the mic.

If hate were a weapon, how many people would you have killed?
If injustice were a casket, how many cemeteries filled?
If you knew your words, could have saved a soul,
Would you have uttered them with a different goal?
If you knew your actions, could have changed a life,
Would you have picked out the bad ones and cut 'em with a knife?
If all the time you had, could be spent anywhere,
Would you spend it with your family or the people you hold dear?

If you had all the riches the world had to offer,
Would you spend it all on love and end up a pauper?
If you could go back in time and give your life for another,
Would you give it freely, or would you even bother?
I would.

When I finish, I realize I didn't open my journal.

I make my way back to my seat as people cheer and hoot. I want to look back to where Shepherd is, but my stubborn pride won't let me. He's too busy with Chase anyway to have paid attention to the poem.

Chapter Twelve

SHEPHERD

Evelyn is such a mystery.

The piece she recited last week is still in my head.

I only went to the poetry slam to see if there was something going on between her and Elliot. But then she went on that stage.

Her poem has me wanting to explore her mind, find out what makes Evelyn, *Evelyn*. Find out what happened in her past, what regrets she has. If that poem is any indication, there are things she wishes she could go back and change.

I want to know what they are.

"Who's she?" Evelyn asks, pointing to a family photo I have of my birth mother.

It's the only photo I have of her, period. In it, she and dad are standing behind a three-year-old version of me as she pushes me on a kiddie swing. We're all laughing in the photo. Those were the happier times. Times I have very little recollection of.

I don't know why I kept the photo. My mother left us. That should've made me hate her, should've made me take the photo and, I don't know, destroy it like she did our family when she left.

I hadn't though.

"She's my biological mother."

Judging by the confused look on her face, I explain that Jackie is actually my stepmom.

"Oh, that's your *mom* mom," she says, observing the photo through narrowed eyes before reaching for it. "I can see the resemblance. The hair, the eyes."

"*Mom* is reserved for the ones who are actually *in* your life. *She* gave birth to me, stuck around for five years and then jumped ship. So, yeah."

I take the frame from her hands and put it back on the shelf.

"Wow," she says.

It's gotten so easy to talk to her that I didn't realize how heavy and sad my story might seem to her. She's got two parents who actually give a damn.

"Have you ever tried looking for her, you know, to find out why she left?"

"Uh, no," I respond without hesitation.

I was young when my mother left us, but if you ask me, she left us long before she was gone. I don't have memories of crying or even missing her.

Dad has been with a slew of women over the years. Jackie came not so long ago, and was with my dad for a while before they got married. Although she isn't competing for mother-of-the-year, she isn't cruel. I get along with her. And that was, and *is*, good enough for me.

"Just '*no*.' You never tried to contact her? Not even to find out why she left your dad?"

"And me," I add. "You forget the part where she left her kid behind like I was some kind of burden she didn't want to deal with."

"Shepherd, you were a kid then. At that age you wouldn't have been able to understand what went on between adults behind closed doors."

"Look, I get it. But I don't think there's an excuse for leaving your kid behind."

Pursing her lips, she decides not to pursue it any further. I want to think it's because she gets my point. But with Evelyn, it's probably because she sees I won't budge, and doesn't want to argue.

Nudging her in the side, I say, "Hey, not everyone has a perfect family. Count yourself lucky that the folks you love actually stuck around."

Her body immediately goes rigid. She looks over at the old family photo we've been discussing, and for several seconds she just sits there staring at it, unblinking.

"Hey," I whisper, snapping my fingers in front of her eyes. "Where'd you go?"

Blinking several times, she shifts her gaze back to me. "What?"

"What were you thinking about just then?"

"Nothing," she answers, looking away as she moves to stand.

"No, not 'nothing,'" I say, preventing her from getting up, my hand on her thigh.

Keeping her eyes averted, she looks over at the door.

"Is it my dad?" I ask, remembering back to when he'd caught her in his office. He hadn't been the most welcoming.

"What? No. Why would you even think that?" She's

almost defensive, tripping over her words as she refocuses her attention to me.

"I don't know. I saw you look over at the door so I thought maybe you were thinking—"

"No. I wasn't thinking about your dad," she states, her voice tense.

"He doesn't hate you, you know. He gets into his moods sometimes when he's super stressed."

Reaching for her books where she'd left them in a pile on my bed, she motions for me to get my laptop. "We need to actually get work done tonight. Your essay isn't going to write itself."

"Aw, Ev, and here I thought you were gonna be awesome enough to write it for me."

"Shepherd, I offered to tutor you, not to do the work for you. There's a difference."

"A guy can dream." I grab the laptop.

It takes us the next two hours, but I finally have my history essay in the bag.

"Yes!" I groan out in victory.

Evelyn's phone vibrates where she has it faceup on my bed. I'm nosy so I sneak a glance at her phone screen as she looks over to read the text.

Jones.

Of course.

He's asking if she wants to go see a movie.

Irritated, I turn away and feign interest in my printer as it works to produce my essay. The more time they spend together, the more annoyed I get because it's not like I can ask her not to hang out with him.

I want her to stay a little longer.

"Hey, I'm heading out," she says after looking up from her phone.

I can't stand the idea that when she leaves here, she's going to go see Jones, so I blurt, "Did you want to hang out for a bit? I was thinking we could watch a movie, or you know, just hang out."

Yeah. That's the only bright idea I can come up with.

Excitement level?

Zero.

Possibility of her saying yes?

None.

I'm losing my touch. I know how to show a girl a good time, so what kind of counteroffer was that?

As I stand there mentally punishing myself, I'm shocked when she replies, "Sure. What kind of movies do you like?"

I stand staring at her like a clown, before my R2-D2 brain sputters back into speech. "Um—uh. Yeah, so I like action. *Star Wars. Mission Impossible.*"

I give you exhibit A.

When I hear myself, I start to question where my balls disappeared to.

"I like action too, but I don't think it even comes close to movies that make you question reality," she says.

"Ahh, so you're into stuff like *Inception*? I dig that," I say honestly. "What movie would you say is the best of all time?"

"Oh wow, that's *literally* impossible to answer," she replies, eyes wide. "You can choose a favorite movie?"

"Yeah. *Mission Impossible: Fallout.* Hands down."

"Ooh, yeah that was really good."

"I have the whole series. Are you down?" I offer, unable to rein in my excitement.

"Are you kidding? Let's go!"

I walk us down to my huge home theatre in the basement, and when we get there, I grin in pride as she surveys the room. It has dark wood-paneled walls and dimmable lighting. The screen on the back wall is about two hundred inches in length, and complete with surround sound. It makes the room seem even more enormous. I motion to the L-shaped recliner and ask if she wants anything to eat.

"Can we order pizza?" she asks.

"On it."

After I get her topping choices, I order for us and go up to the kitchen to grab a couple of sodas. I jump when I see my dad perched on the edge of one of the barstools by the kitchen island.

"When'd you get here?" I didn't hear the garage door, or any other sounds from him entering the house.

"I'm not staying. I parked in the driveway. We have a business social tonight. Jackie's idea not mine," he says.

"Well, you know Jackie's all about appearances. Listen, I have Evelyn over. We finished school stuff and now we're getting ready to watch some movies downstairs."

His face changes. He puts on that cautionary expression he wears when I mention spending time with a girl. "Shepherd," he starts.

"I know, I know. But you don't have to worry about that." There is definitely nothing like that going on between us.

"Hmm," he snorts. "Whatever you do, you'd better make damned sure you use protection. I don't plan on being a grandfather anytime soon." Looking at me sternly, he pockets his cell phone, gets up from the stool and strolls toward his office.

Side-eyeing him as he walks away, I go to the fridge, grab the drinks, then head back down to Evelyn.

"Thanks," she says as she reaches for the Coke I hand her. "Did something happen?"

"Nah. My dad's here is all. I told him you were over."

She tenses up at the mention of my dad.

"I told you. You don't have to worry about him." I knew she was thinking about him earlier when she told me it was nothing.

"And I told *you* it wasn't your father I was thinking about."

"Oh? Then what was it?"

She looks away.

"See. You can't even tell me."

"Are we gonna watch the movie or not?"

"Are you gonna tell me what's up?"

"No," she says flatly, rising to her feet.

"OK, OK. Let's watch the movie." I sit and pull her down next to me.

I navigate the movie menu until I find the first installment of the *Mission Impossible* series.

Almost two hours and a box of pizza later, the movie ends and we're both hooked. You'd think we'd never watched it before. We decide on following up with the second installment. While I set it up, Evelyn heads up to use the bathroom.

When I realize she's gone for a longer time than expected, I go upstairs in search of her. I frown when I knock on the door of the bathroom closest to us and no one answers. When I push open the door and step inside to check, she's not in there.

That's odd. Why would she not use this one?

"Ev?" I say out loud as I turn to leave the bathroom. "Ev!" I yell a little louder when I receive no response.

When I hear quiet footsteps, I turn in the direction they're coming from.

"What is it?" she asks.

"Where were you?"

"What do you mean? I went to the bathroom."

"There's one right here," I say eyeing her, trying to figure out if she didn't see the bathroom by the stairs.

"How was I supposed to know what that room was? The door was closed. I only know the one by your room and by that office," she explains, pointing behind her. "And I wasn't gonna go *all* the way upstairs to avoid bumping into your dad."

"I *knew* it. You *were* thinking about my dad," I say with a smirk. "I told you he gets like that sometimes. He wasn't taking offense at you. He's cagey and doesn't like people being in his space. Trust me, Ev, he holds nothing against you," I add. I don't want her feeling like she has to walk on eggshells every time Dad's around. "He's not here, he had someplace else to be."

"I understand," she says without hesitation. "Come on let's go watch the movie."

"Uh ... OK." I get the feeling something's off, but I have no idea what it is. I turn around and head back downstairs, Evelyn behind me.

It's a little after nine when the movie ends, and even though I selfishly want to watch the next one with her, I need to take her home. We have school tomorrow and I don't want to be the reason she can't stay awake in her classes.

"We should do this again sometime," I say as we walk to my car.

"Yeah, I'll let you know." She slips into the passenger

seat, tugging twice on her seat belt once she secures it. This isn't the first time I've seen her do it.

"Why do you do that?" I ask.

Puzzled, she looks over at me. "Do what?"

I tug twice on my seat belt in emphasis.

"I've done it ever since my br—" She cuts herself off mid-sentence and then adds, "I don't know. Out of habit I guess."

"And why do you do *that*?"

"Do what?"

"Get all cagey when I ask you personal stuff. You're just like my dad." She is in that sense.

"I'm nothing like your father," she counters, looking away from me and through the windshield.

I frown because I don't know how to feel about the way she said that. I mean, I agree. She's nothing like my father in other ways. But she becomes heavily guarded whenever I try to ask her anything beyond surface-level questions.

I pull out of my driveway and head to her house.

We ride in semi-silence. I want to talk about other things besides school, and anytime I ask about her child-hood, she clams up, answering me with just so much and not enough. At one point I get so frustrated, I stop talking altogether. After that, we ride in silence until we get to her place. I realize she may need more time to warm up to me and that's OK. I can be patient.

When I kill the engine and attempt to get out of the car and walk her to the door, she places a hand on my arm. "Shepherd, you don't need to do that. Thanks for the ride, and for tonight."

That's another thing I don't get. I don't mind giving her a ride, but I know her parents have money. How come she doesn't have a car? I know it's pointless asking her because she won't answer that. At least not now.

"I mean it. I enjoyed spending time with you tonight," she says, her gaze on mine.

"Me too," I say in agreement.

She hesitates for a second.

I swear I'm going crazy or something because I think she's contemplating kissing me.

Wait, scratch that.

Nah. Negative. Not possible.

I need to get my imagination in check because there's no way Evelyn is interested in me like that. It's a miracle she doesn't hate my guts right now for all I've done to her since we met.

Instead, she squeezes my arm and then gets out of the car.

"Have a good night, Shepherd. Drive safely." Waving at me, she turns and walks to her front door. She opens it and gives me one last smile before closing it behind her.

Letting out a breath I didn't realize I'd been holding, I stare at her front door. Backing out of her driveway, I start on the long, lonely journey back home.

Chapter Thirteen

I get to Shepherd's place a little earlier than scheduled. He's still at practice and his dad isn't here yet, which gives me plenty of time to go through with what I have planned.

I find the spare key in the flower box and enter his house. I waste no time making a beeline for his dad's office, and planting the camera in the position I'd already checked out. The camera in place; I check my watch. Mr. Buchanan should be home in the next fifteen minutes or so.

I go across the hall to the bathroom and check my appearance in the mirror. I plump my lips and put on the ruby-red lipstick I brought with me. I adjust my too-short skirt and crop top.

Sometime later, when I hear the garage door, I sprint to the living room and take a seat on the sofa, pulling out a book.

"Good afternoon, Evelyn," he says, noticing how my legs are scantily covered by the thin material of my skirt.

"Hi, Mr. Buchanan."

He heads straight to his office.

I give it about another ten minutes, enough time for him to get settled in. With any luck he's already taken a few sips of the alcohol he keeps in his office.

I get up and quietly walk to his office door. After peeking in, I push the door open.

"Mr. Buchanan?"

"Yes?"

I step in, closing the door behind me. "I have a question."

He gets up from his chair and rounds the desk, leaning against it, his arms folded. "Before you ask, I have one of my own. Do you think it is appropriate to wear such revealing clothes around my son?" He points at my outfit.

I move closer to him, and he looks at me, amused. "What exactly did you want to ask me, *young* lady?"

I shift my gaze from his vivid blue eyes down to his lips. I strengthen my resolve to go through with everything.

As I push into his personal space, he unfolds his arms and stands taller. "What do you think you're doing?"

I place my arms on his shoulders and bring my mouth up to his, covering it. I attempt to make the whole thing appear as natural as possible, as if we've done this before.

For a few seconds he's shocked, because he doesn't move. He then encircles my upper arms and pulls me off of him.

I try to do it again but he holds me away from him. "Evelyn, you're mistaken. I don't mess with minors, let alone little *girls* attending my son's school."

When I pretend to be disappointed, he continues. "You know, I had a feeling you had an adolescent crush on me, but I didn't think you would take it this far. I'll only say this once." He puts me away from him and releases my arms. "I will not permit you to enter my home if this ever happens again. Do you understand me?"

I nod, looking down at the floor. I need him to leave so I can get my camera. I try to look distraught and regretful in hopes he'll give me a moment of privacy.

"Right. Well, I'll leave you to think about the actions you've taken here this evening. They should never, *ever* be repeated. I hope I made myself clear." He bypasses me and exits the room.

I'm grateful. I grab my camera, hit the stop button, then retrieve my bag from where I'd left it.

I head up to Shepherd's room and change out of the barely there outfit and prepare for our session. Knowing Mr. Buchanan, he won't tell Shepherd what happened. I relax until Shepherd comes.

About twenty minutes later, Shepherd pushes into the bedroom. I jump up from the bed, a little more eager than I usually am.

"Hey!"

"*Hey* to you too." He chuckles. "What's gotten you so excited? And don't tell me it's anything other than the prospect of seeing this handsome face."

"You wish."

"I do," he says, throwing me off with how honest he sounds. "Listen, a group of us are going up to Tallulah this weekend if you're free."

"Yeah, Jones was telling me about it. I can come up with you guys for Friday, but someone'll have to drop me home Saturday afternoon."

"How come?"

"Family plans."

"And of course, you won't tell me any more than that."

"It's a dinner we've had every Saturday night since—since we hardly spend time together during the week," I lie. If I tell Shepherd about Ethan, he's going to start asking questions. And if I answer those questions, he'll definitely end up putting two and two together.

I can't risk that.

"That's cool," he replies. "Hey, look at this." He takes out an assignment from his bag and hands it to me. It's the essay for history we worked on about two weeks ago. There's a solid A at the top of the paper. I can see how proud he is of himself, and I can't help but smile up at him.

"You're a miracle worker, Ev." He places his lips against my cheek in a brief kiss.

For a few seconds, I'm so stunned I don't know how to react.

"That's all you, Shepherd, I'm only here to help." I'm grateful when my voice doesn't betray the awkwardness I feel.

"Agree to disagree." He reaches for the assignment and his hand covers mine for the briefest of seconds.

I instantly look up at him, but he's already pulling out his textbook, making it difficult for me to gauge his features.

I'm overthinking things.

"Alright, let's start," he says, smacking his hand down over the textbook cover.

The sound jerks me out of my thoughts, and I go over to sit with him.

When we're about halfway through with the session, Shepherd's dad knocks on his bedroom door.

My heart flies into my throat, and my anxiety levels rise.

"Shep?" Mr. Buchanan calls out from the other side of the door.

"Yeah, Dad? What's up?" Shepherd opens the door and steps out.

"I need to speak with you for a moment before I go."

Shepherd pulls the door closed behind him.

I shoot up and tiptoe over to it, straining my ear to hear what they're saying. I can't decipher anything because they're not standing by the door. I walk back into the room and stand staring over at it.

I don't know if I expect Shepherd to come barging in demanding what the hell I did with his father, but when the door opens again, I jump.

"What did he say?" I ask.

"Nothing much. He said Jackie'll be here soon, and something about telling her he went out for a bit."

I'm relieved but try to act nonchalant.

"Ev? Did something happen with you?"

When he asks me that, my eyes widen with alarm. "Wh—what do you mean?"

He's quiet for a moment, contemplating.

"The poem. The one you recited at that poetry slam thing."

I'm so freaking grateful that it's something else, I answer without a second thought. "Yeah, but it was a long time ago."

"What was it?" he asks as he sits on the bed and pats a spot next to him for me to join.

I sit next to him. "Not much really." I bring my bottom lip between my teeth. It's not a complete lie. *I* wasn't the one who died that night. "I just wish I could go back and change a few things. That's all."

"Cage meet Evelyn." He makes a makeshift circle with one hand and brings two fingers of the other through it. "There you go again being all cagey. It's your past anyway and I'm not rushing the process. I guess when you trust me more, you'll tell me more."

"Is that what you think? That I'll trust you more?" I can't help but laugh at the irrational expectation. I shake my head, because nothing could be further from reality.

I could *never* trust him.

He looks over at me and something shifts in his gaze. Then he reaches down and grabs his textbook.

A few hours later, I'm back home and putting the SD card in my laptop to check out the footage. When I see how clear the recording is, I'm so freaking happy I almost start doing a victory dance.

I got the bastard.

Mr. Buchanan wouldn't be getting off no matter how hard he tried to spin it this time.

Now I need to edit the video down, remove the volume and move on to phase two of my plan. The first phase, which is to get Mr. Buchanan charged with illicit relations with a minor, can only be completed after the next phase.

Shepherd Buchanan.

I've gotten a great start on everything, and I'm pretty impressed with how well things are going. I have a feeling Shepherd is into me, but I'm not 100 percent sure yet.

I'm not a heartless bitch, but I think the part of me that was capable of real love died along with my brother.

My motive for doing this is fueled by one thing: the unbending need to see the person who killed my brother pay. And that, by any means necessary.

"Dad." I find my dad in the kitchen as he and Mom are preparing dinner. Today they're both in at a reasonable hour.

Good.

"Oh yay, you're both here. I have to run something by you guys."

"What is it, sweetheart?" Dad asks, looking over his shoulder.

"How was school?" my mom asks.

"It was OK today, nothing special happened," I reply. "Hey, a few of the kids are going up to Tallulah Falls for the weekend. Can I go? I'll be sure to be back before evening on Saturday."

"Who's driving?" my dad asks. He pauses dicing a tomato for the salad he's making and turns to face me.

"Tiffany or Jones, but I'm not sure yet."

He looks over at Mom and the two of them nod, then he turns to me. "Sure, you may go." If he only knew what Jones had planned those weeks ago, I don't think he'd be OK with Jones taking me anywhere.

"Yay! Thank you, Daddy," I say, excited. "What's for dinner?"

"Well your dad ordered sushi for him and me but since we know you don't like it, we decided to make baked ziti for you."

"Fine. Call me when dinner's ready."

When I get back to my room, I call up Tiffany, letting her know I can go to Tallulah. I question her about the plans for this weekend. Apparently, the boys take the lead on what activities we do. We'll be sleeping in tents, so I have to pack light.

"It's going to be fun, trust me. Oh and wear a swimsuit. We're probably getting in the water as soon as we get there."

"Did you guys decide on who's driving?" I ask.

"I'm driving. Casey is riding with Jones."

"That's cool. Do you know who all's going?"

"Well, let's see. Most of the football players will go. Some people from the lacrosse and swim teams. A few of the cheerleaders, Beanca, Chase." She continues naming some other people I don't know, but I stop paying attention after she says Chase's name. I should have known she would be there. I don't have anything against the girl. I just hope she doesn't become a monkey wrench in my plan.

Chapter Fourteen

EVIE

Tallulah Falls is beautiful.

Tiffany parks while I take in everything, staring up at the trees towering above us. Their vibrant green leaves dance in the wind. My gaze shifts to the hills and hiking trails in the distance, and I spot a small waterfall peeking out of a hidden ravine.

"I have to come up here more often." The verdant landscape has me hooked.

"We're here at least twice a month. You can always come with," Jones says, getting the equipment from the trunk of his car. He pulled in just minutes before we did. Casey circles around to help him, while Tiffany pulls her bag from the back seat and comes to stand with me.

We follow a trail down to the river to meet up with the others there. The moment we get to the riverbank, I notice Shepherd is already here with Chase.

Of course.

Beanca, Lucas, and John are here too, along with a

handful of other players from the football team. There are a few other faces I don't recognize.

"Jones, you finally made it," Shepherd says in greeting. "Evelyn, Tiffany, Casey. Hey."

"Hey," we all say in unison.

Moments later, people start stripping down to their swimsuits and diving off into the river.

I reach for the hem of my T-shirt and lift it over my head. My yellow string bikini top almost comes loose at the motion, and I quickly secure it, retightening the knot at the nape of my neck. I keep my khaki shorts on over my bikini bottom because I don't need any accidents happening with that too. If I'd thought better I would have worn a sturdier set.

When I look up, I notice Shepherd turning his head away. He's already removed his shirt, and the muscles of his back ripple when he bends to pick up a water gun.

One of the first activities is a girls versus guys water gun fight.

Shepherd hands the water gun to Chase and gets another for Beanca. Then he picks one out for himself.

Jones goes to grab us a few.

Removing my sandals, I leave my water gun on the bank and wade in, splashing cool water against my skin and face. Tiffany joins me, floating on the surface for a bit.

Jones gets in and immediately starts splashing us. He comes after me, tackling me in the water.

He and Casey plan a quick game. He places me over his shoulder, my legs around his neck, and Casey does the same with Tiffany. We start wrestling each other to see who will knock the other over first.

When I knock her over, she tips Casey over too. We're all dying of laughter when they both disappear under the water, only to reappear a few seconds later coughing and bickering at each other.

"You guys ready?" Shepherd yells over from the river's bank.

"Yeah, we're coming," Jones says, wading back.

We all follow him, heading back and filling up our water guns.

Chase comes up behind Shepherd, placing her arms around his waist.

I pull my eyes away.

We're ready to start after a few minutes, and Lucas attempts to shell out some rules.

"Ain't no rules to a water gun fight, Lucas," John says. "They just need to get back here without getting sprayed. Let's start the game. We'll give the girls a few seconds head start. That's it."

The guys do a countdown, while we run as fast and as far away from them as we can. At first, there's a large group of us girls. Then someone suggests we all separate to make it harder for the boys to find us. I end up with Tiffany, but we ditch each other soon after.

This has to be *the* most intense water gun fight I've ever been a part of. It's more like a hunt.

I stop at one of the pine trees at the edge of a path, trying to catch my breath. The path leads into an even denser crowd of trees, and I contemplate going back the way I came.

I whip around at the sudden spray of water on my hand where it rests against the tree trunk.

I spot Shepherd, coming after me with his gun aimed. I immediately take off into a sprint. I eventually lose him and end up hiding behind a huge shrub.

He stalks by, intent on finding me.

I stare at him through the bushes.

I can see why girls are into him, why Chase wants him. He looks good, and it's obvious he knows it. There's a certain charm about him. His curly blond hair makes him look boyish at times. At other times, his body exudes this strong, masculine appeal.

Wait. *What?*

When I realize where my thoughts are going, I refocus my attention on the game. I need to get out from behind these bushes and head back to the starting point without getting caught in the crossfire.

Thinking Shepherd is gone, I creep out from my hiding spot.

I don't get far before I hear the telltale movements of someone up ahead.

What the hell? How did he—?

I instantly turn toward the direction of the woods and take off like my life depends on it.

I hear his laughter behind me. "You can run, but there ain't no hiding from me." He attempts to squirt water at me but misses several times.

I'm determined, running in zigzag patterns to avoid the sprays.

He chases after me, forcing us deeper into the woods.

I bring myself up short, dropping my water gun and jumping back. There's a red and black snake slithering in the grass ahead. I slowly start walking backward, all thoughts of the game fleeing my mind.

Shepherd comes up behind me, squirting water at my back. "Hey!" He playfully slides an arm around my waist. "Got you."

I don't think. I whirl and pounce on him, bringing both legs up, and wrapping myself around him.

"Whoa, what is it?" He looks over my shoulder, holding me against him.

When he spots the snake, he brings his other arm up and shoots water at it.

A few seconds pass and he doesn't say anything.

"Shepherd, is it gone?"

I take my head from his shoulder and twist around to see if the snake is still there. It's not. I search the ground a few yards ahead and still don't see any sign of it. Relieved, I turn back around. My eyes connect with Shepherd's.

His eyes have darkened to a deep sapphire. I don't realize how much I've noticed his eyes until now.

His gaze shifts to my mouth.

I hesitate when he brings his face closer, resting his forehead against mine. He presses his lips to my mouth, softly at first. At the contact, a current courses through me. My skin becomes sensitive, and I can feel him almost everywhere.

He drops the water gun, then smooths the palms of his hands on the skin of my back, pressing me to him. I comb shaky fingers through his hair, returning his kiss.

"Evelyn," Shepherd whispers against my mouth. "What are we doing?"

I don't want to think about what we're doing. I focus on his lips, placing kisses at the corners of his mouth.

Taking that as some sort of hint, Shepherd starts kissing me again, with more confidence this time. He places an index finger against my mouth as his eyes search mine. "I've been wanting to do this, to kiss you."

I bring my legs down from around his waist, and he immediately hugs me to him. I feel out of sorts, and it's as if I don't know what's come over me. My face feels heated, and his is also flushed.

"You're so beautiful, Evelyn," he says, staring into my

eyes. Lowering his head, he puts his mouth on mine and frames my face in his hands.

We stay here like this, completely taken over by the heat of the moment.

"Shepherd!"

"Evie!"

I'm brought back to reality when people call for us. It's Tiffany, and a few other people.

I break the kiss and push at Shepherd to let me go. When he does, I fix myself. He picks up his discarded water gun and holds it in front of him.

I hurry ahead, pretending he's still chasing me through the trees.

"I'm here!" I yell. "Run! He's loaded." I push at Tiffany to turn around, and she's immediately in full sprint.

I don't think about what Shepherd and I did.

In fact, I try to put it out of my mind for the rest of the trip.

SHEPHERD

Evelyn runs off, and I watch her.

I can't get what just happened out of my head.

She let me hold her, kiss her, and it has my head reeling. The way she was with me leaves no doubt in my mind that Evelyn is interested in me. I thought she might be attracted to me, but thought I was imagining it.

I touch a hand to my mouth.

"Shepherd, there you are, dude," Lucas says, rushing over. He's flanked by Chase and Beanca.

The girls both scream as they start squirting their water guns at us. I raise mine and Lucas turns on them too. We spray them as they run ahead of us.

When we all finally get back to the river, it's almost dark. Everyone packs their stuff and heads to our designated campsite for the night.

My eyes travel to Evelyn where she's standing in a group with Casey and Tiffany.

Moments later, we get to the campgrounds. Tiffany and Evelyn decide to share a tent with a few other girls, while Jones, Lucas, John, and I share one. A few others in our group decide on co-ed tents, especially those who're already coupled up.

We build up the campfire and bring out the hot dogs and marshmallows. A cooler filled with ice, water, and other drinks is set at a distance. People set up their portable chairs and we all sit around the fire.

To my left is Chase, then Lucas. On my right is Beanca, followed by Jones, then Evelyn. I'm bummed that Evelyn's seated so far away, but I can't do anything about it without raising suspicion.

We all make s'mores, while Lucas starts in on the stories.

"So this one time when we were kids, Shepherd had this girl in middle school who was crushing on him hard," he says. I look over at him with the *are-you-serious-dude?* face. Of course he ignores it. "Anyway, he told the girl that liking him was pointless because he would never be with only one girl. She calls him a cheater and he goes, 'I can't cheat if I was never with you now can I?' The poor girl was heartbroken, and Shepherd never batted an eye."

"And it's been that way ever since, huh?" Chase asks, laughing as she caresses my hand where it rests on my knee.

I instantly look over at Evelyn, whose gaze is trained on Chase's hand. I lift my hand, causing Chase's to fall away.

Evelyn looks up at me, then away, staring into the campfire.

I want to know what she's thinking, if she cares that Chase held my hand, how she felt about it.

"Jones is like that too," Beanca adds, bringing my attention to her as she looks over at him. "He's never with one girl, even if he makes it out like he is. Isn't that right?" She pats him on the thigh and then shifts her gaze to Evelyn.

Hmm.

I want to ask Beanca why she thought it necessary to make the comment, but I don't.

"When I'm committed, I'm committed, Bee. Don't try to throw me under with Shepherd."

"I take offense at that," I chime in, narrowing my eyes at him.

"The truth can do that sometimes," Jones replies.

"Speaking of, Beanca what happened to Beverly?" Rachael, one of the cheerleaders, asks. "She tried out for the team and after decisions were made, she stopped coming around."

"She wasn't hanging with us all that much," Beanca responds.

"She would've been here now though. Is she OK?"

I notice Jones's look of irritation and wonder what that's all about.

"It's a shame she didn't make the team. Girl is gorgeous!" John pipes up.

"Oh shut up! As if you would've been able to get anywhere near my sister." Beanca glares at him. He shrugs, looking over at Lexie, who's currently sitting on some dude's lap. A muscle twitches in his jaw.

Hmm.

Like me, John doesn't really *do* relationships. He's

messed around with so many girls, I don't put it past him for Lexie to have been one of his conquests. I'm not proud of the fact that I've messed around with her because Lexie's a messy chick. She knows it, owns up to it.

I haven't reached out to her in a minute and I don't plan to.

"You're so *cute* when you do that, Lex," the guy says to her as she giggles and tugs at his hair.

John gets up then, letting us know he's got to go relieve himself.

"TMI, Johnny boy, TMI," Rachael says.

"I have an idea," Chase chimes in. "Why don't we play a game of truth or dare?" She wears a wicked but playful grin on her face as she looks around at everyone.

"Great minds think alike, because I was just about to pitch that," Lucas adds. He then proceeds to lay out some basic ground rules for the game.

"I'll go first. Shepherd, truth or dare?" Chase looks at me with a wily smile.

"Come on, why'd you have to start with me?" I ask, reluctant.

"Because ... why not?"

"Alright. Truth."

"Ugh. Booooring." She glares at me and continues when she realizes I'm not changing my mind. "Fine. Is it true that you only go for blondes?"

"Generally speaking, but that doesn't prevent me from being attracted to other chicks." I want to see how Evelyn's taking this, but all eyes are on me and if I even glance her way, they'll notice.

"I'll go next—" Beanca starts, but Lucas interrupts her.

"Rules, Bee. You can't go until you're asked. Shepherd's next."

I look at Beanca's sullen face.

"Beanca, truth or dare?" I ask.

She smiles wide, almost giddy. "Dare."

"I dare you to kiss Lucas." I know, I'm sick, but we're all friends here.

"What? No. I don't want to kiss Lucas," she complains. "Are you serious?"

"It's not like I'm over here dying to kiss you either, *princess*." Lucas side-eyes her and brings the marshmallow he'd been melting to his mouth.

"You chose dare. You gotta do it, or else the game ends here," I deadpan.

She immediately gets up, goes over to Lucas and gives him a quick peck on his cheek before returning to her chair.

"There."

"Wow, you call that a kiss?" Lucas asks, chewing on his marshmallow.

"He never said what kind of kiss it had to be. So don't come for me."

"Whatever." Lucas proceeds to stick another marshmallow on the skewer in his hand before placing it over the flames.

"Anyway, my turn. Truth or dare?" Beanca asks, looking to her right at Jones.

"Easy. Dare."

Beanca is silent for a few seconds, then says, "I dare you ... to make out with Evelyn."

Everyone looks between Jones and Evelyn, then at Beanca. The fire crackles and a familiar heat rises up my neck.

When Jones starts leaning in toward Evelyn, my hand curls into a fist. As soon as Evelyn's hand touches his upper arm, I blurt, "What the hell is this? The kissing game? I thought we were playing truth or dare. Is everyone gonna be dared to kiss someone else?"

All eyes train on me, including Jones and Evelyn's, whom I've successfully prevented from locking lips.

"You're one to talk, dude," Lucas says, smirking at me.

"And what the hell's that supposed to mean?"

"Shep, in all honesty, you started it when you dared me to kiss Lucas," Beanca defends.

"Yeah, well, then you should come up with something *original*, since the kiss trope has already been used."

"I'm not changing my dare," she says, glowering at me before turning her attention back to Jones and Evelyn. "Proceed."

The whole thing is awkward now and I can tell that Evelyn is uncomfortable.

"No," Jones says after he too realizes Evelyn's discomfort. "The moment's gone. Truth."

"You can't change back to truth after choosing dare," Beanca states.

"Which rule is that?" Lucas asks.

"The obvious one."

"Actually, I made up the rules and I didn't say no takebacks," Lucas argues.

They bicker across the fire at each other. I stop listening to them when I notice Evelyn saying something to Tiffany. She gets up and walks over to their tent.

A few other people start talking to each other, and I glance around.

"I'll be right back," I say, excusing myself.

A few seconds later, I'm standing in front of Evelyn's tent flap. "Hey," I whisper.

Evelyn startles. "Shepherd? What are you doing here?"

"We need to talk."

"About what?"

I walk away from the tent and wait. After a moment, she emerges. She looks around, finally sees me, and heads over.

We're near the trees and out of everyone's view.

"What is it?" she asks, looking behind her to make sure no one can see us.

"Why'd you kiss me earlier?" Yeah, not subtle at all.

She pauses for a second and then looks up at me. "Why did *you* kiss *me*? If you answer me, then I'll answer you."

Of course.

"Because I'm attracted to you."

"Exactly. And that's why I kissed you. It's not a big deal, so don't worry about it. You can keep whatever you have going on with Chase," she says motioning behind her. "We can pretend it didn't happen," she finishes, then averts her gaze.

Pretend it didn't happen?

My mood sours further when she adds, "It was fun though," before walking back to the tent.

I frown, watching her retreat.

I hesitate before striding back to the circle at the campfire, confused at why her flippancy over what happened between us gets to me.

It was fun though.

That's what it was to her? Something *fun* she did to pass the time? She let me kiss her like that, and it was just ... *fun?* With Lexie or Chase, or any other chick for that matter, wasn't that what it was?

Fun?

So why the hell does it piss me off that Evelyn thought the same?

"Shep, you good, bro?" Jones asks.

My mind is so muddled I didn't notice anyone was talking to me. "Yeah, what's up?"

"John and Lucas are wondering if you noticed Dudley acting weird lately. I mean, he didn't come up with us this time and he never misses these Tallulah trips," Jones says.

Dudley has been a pain in my ass for the past few weeks. I've chalked it up to stress. Coach has been running us ragged during practice for the final games of the season.

"I noticed."

"He's probably just high-strung because around this time we have all these exams and shit. Plus, Coach has been on him," John offers, looking at us to confirm his theory.

"Makes sense," Lucas says with a shrug.

"Whatever it is, he needs to *re-lax*." I've taken one too many hard hits from him out on the field during practice, and we're on the same team.

"We should all do that, *relax*," John says, looking over at Lexie. The guy she'd been sitting on must have excused himself, because I notice he's no longer present. She rolls her eyes at John, then stares out into the darkness.

"Speaking of, I'm turning in," I say.

"This early? No, Shep, *stay*. Please," Chase begs, grabbing hold of my hand.

I shake my head.

When she releases me, I walk over to the tent I'm sharing with the guys. I'm too distracted right now and wouldn't be much for company anyway.

Chapter Fifteen

EVIE

It's been two weeks since the Tallulah trip, and I've been canceling my sessions with Shepherd ever since.

I'm getting in my own way.

When he mentioned having a type during the trip, I was upset that I let him kiss me. The way Chase is with him, how familiar they are with each other, I shouldn't let it affect me.

But it does.

This thing with Shepherd needs to be one-sided for it to work out how I intend it to. I shouldn't be *feeling* anything. I can work with attraction. Anything beyond that, anything involving my emotions, needs to be flushed out and fast.

I've been distant with Shepherd, giving him one-word answers when he texts me. At school, I keep our conversations brief. They say absence makes the heart grow fonder, so if I blow cold long enough, maybe he'll bite.

I'm in history, and Mrs. Walker is finishing up a lecture on the American Revolutionary War. She gives us a mini project where we have to pair up with someone, one of us has to be the redcoat, and the other, blue. The redcoats represent the British Army, while the bluecoats are the Continental.

Elliot comes over, choosing me as his partner. I want to be a bluecoat. He argues that France helped the colonies during the American Revolution, that his family is from there, so it's only fitting he gets to be a bluecoat.

We argue until he gives up.

"OK, I raise the white flag. You win. Come on." He grabs hold of my arm and hauls me to the front, where Mrs. Walker is giving out the instructions and project cards.

I chuckle because the Americans actually did win the war. When I grab for a card from one of the piles, a hand covers mine. I'm not surprised to see it's Shepherd's. I try to pick up the card anyway and attempt to bring my hand out from under his, but he presses down, trapping me.

I don't do anything, but stand with my gaze averted. Other people come up to collect cards from the pile, and he reaches under our hands, picks them up and hands them out.

Elliot comes over after getting the packet of instructions from Mrs. Walker. When he sees my hand trapped under Shepherd's, he gives us a confused look.

"What's going on?" he asks.

"You tell me, Elliot," Shepherd says, scowling at him. "What's going on with you and Evelyn?"

When Elliot looks uncomfortable, I answer, my gaze now on my project partner. "It's none of his business what goes on between us, Elliot. He's choosing to be a jerk because he can."

Shepherd brings his mouth to my ear. "Did I do something to piss you off? Tell me what it is and I'll fix it. But *stop* ignoring me."

And ... he bites.

I turn to face him then. "Let's talk about it later."

"Later when?"

"*Later*, after our session."

"Well, seeing as you've been canceling, I didn't think you—"

"I'm not canceling today then. I'll be there," I confirm.

He looks at me like he doubts it.

"I'll be there," I repeat.

He slowly lets go of my hand, then glares at Elliot before getting his project card and heading back to his seat.

I get to Shepherd's house hours after school gets out and notice his car in the driveway. We had to push back the session. I forgot I'd promised my mom I'd help her pick out a wedding gift for one of my cousins who's getting married next weekend.

By the time she drops me at Shepherd's place, it's already a bit dark out.

"He's dropping you home, right?"

"Yeah, Mom." I'm still in my school uniform because I didn't get a chance to go home and change. Mom picked me up as soon as school let out.

"Are his parents home?"

"I think so. They usually park in the garage so chances are at least one of them is in." I know she's asking because she doesn't like the idea of us in the house alone. I've been coming to tutor Shepherd for a while now, and she knows she has nothing to worry about.

"Later." I hurry up the driveway and push the doorbell.

A few seconds go by before Shepherd opens the door.

"I'm sorry. I had to help her pick out a gift."

"No, you're good. Do you want a shirt or something to change into?" he asks, giving me a once-over.

"No, I'm fine." We head up to his room and start the session.

After a full fifteen minutes, I realize Shepherd isn't focused at all.

"OK, what is it? Let's talk about it now because otherwise, this whole hour will be a waste of time for us both."

He shifts his eyes to me, and from the same page he'd been on for the past ten minutes.

When he doesn't say anything, I narrow my gaze. "Why are you just sitting there staring at me? I asked you a question."

"I'm trying to figure you out, Ev," he replies. "Sometimes you're all nice to me, and then other times—I don't know. It's weird."

"Oh, now I'm weird."

"That's not what I said. I said *it's* weird." His gaze turns serious. "Earlier today, you said you'd tell me what's been up with you. I'm all ears."

I face the window. I'm sitting on the edge of his bed, and from where he's lying on his stomach, he can only see my profile.

I'm silent for a beat, then I ask, "Are you and Chase really not together?"

It's so quiet after I ask the question, I could almost believe I'm the only one in the room. Shepherd's body weight causing a depression in the mattress next to me is the only indication I'm not alone. Unable to bear it any longer, I look down at him.

"Ev, are you jealous?" he asks, searching my eyes.

I get up and stalk over to the window. "Of course not! Why would I be jealous? It's not like I like you like that anyway."

I don't even hear him get up. In one stride he's behind me and whirling me around to face him. "Tell me you don't care if I kiss Chase. If I touch her. If I—"

"Shut up, Shepherd! Just shut up OK," I yell, the emotion in my voice foreign to my ears.

I don't know what triggers him. One second I'm yelling at him to shut up, and the next I'm pressed against him and his lips are moving across mine. Stunned, I push at his chest.

When he finally releases me, I slap him, my reflexes getting the better of me.

He looks at me in shock, touching his face where I hit him.

"I'm sorry, but don't do that again," I say, my breathing unsteady. "I refuse to be anyone's second choice."

"Is that what you think?" he asks, eyebrows raised. "You think I'm saying all this, doing all this, because I want to keep Chase and have you as supplement?"

"That's what you did with Lexie. Isn't it? And whatever other girls I don't know about."

He stands there looking at me as if he can't believe what I'm saying.

"Oh come on, it's really not all that surprising that I would think that. And I'm not asking you for anything, so you don't have to *change* anything." I try to go back to the bed in an attempt to salvage the rest of the session. But as soon as I pick up the textbook, he knocks it out of my hand.

"What do you want from me, Evelyn?"

· · ·

SHEPHERD

Evelyn is driving me crazy.

She reaches for the textbook, and again I try to knock it out of her hands. When she manages to hold on to it this time, I take hold of her hand and pry it loose from her fingers, throwing it on the bed.

"What is *wrong* with you? It's getting late and we need to finish."

"Not until you tell me what it is that you want from me. And don't tell me it's nothing because we both know that's bullshit."

"Don't talk to me like that."

"OK fine, how would you like me to talk to you, huh? Would you like me to tell you how I feel about you instead?"

When she doesn't respond, I continue.

"I hate it when you ignore me. At first, I thought you put yourself on some pedestal way above the rest of us. But then I started doing things to piss you off because then you'd react, no matter how hard you tried not to." Her eyes flicker, and I press forward still. "When you warmed up to me and started at least talking to me, I realized I didn't want you pissed at me. I wanted you to like me, be comfortable around me. Only that isn't enough because I'm constantly annoyed when you hang around other guys. I want you to *talk* to me, Evelyn. These past two weeks have been hell not knowing why you stopped wanting to come around me. Why you stopped being how you were with me, canceling our sessions. This thing with Chase means *nothing* to me. I'll drop it if that's what you want. Just talk to me."

The way Evelyn looks at me. I don't think. I immediately capture her mouth again. She doesn't resist, so I deepen the kiss. Parting her lips with my thumb, I touch my tongue to hers.

She reaches her arms up to run her fingers through my hair, then slants her mouth across mine.

My hands slide to the neck of her uniform shirt, working the top buttons free.

Evelyn stops me. "Shepherd, what are you doing?" She's nervous, but there's desire behind her brown eyes.

I don't resist the temptation to seal my mouth to hers again, enjoying the feel of her.

It was fun though.

My jaw clenches at the memory of those words, and I'm wondering if maybe I'm moving too fast with her.

I break the kiss. Opening my eyes, I inhale deeply. "Look at me, Evelyn." I lift her chin, looking into her eyes. "I don't want you to just have fun with me."

I hesitate for the briefest of seconds before bringing my attention to her shirt and buttoning it back up.

Her eyes flicker. "What is it?"

I walk us over to the bed, shove the textbook and other stuff over and sit on the edge. I tug her down next to me. "You said you don't like me, but then you let me kiss you? What are we doing, huh?" When she looks away, I capture one of her hands, interlacing our fingers.

"I ... I was upset. That's all," she says, looking at our hands, the contrast of her tawny skin against my paler one. "I didn't mean it."

"How do you feel about me?" I ask, my heart in my throat.

She's silent for a spell before responding. "You were so rude when I first met you, Shepherd." She smooths the fingers of her free hand over our joined hands. "Cynical, cocky ... aggravating."

"Wow. That bad, huh?" I ask, grinning and nudging her with my thigh.

She laughs, then smacks my leg. "You know it's true."

I can't deny it.

"Truthfully, since I've been tutoring you, hanging out with you, seeing how much we're alike, it made me realize we can be friends."

Friends?

The word echoes in my head.

I frown and my chest heaves. "Do you usually kiss your friends the way you kiss me?" The question sails from my lips before I'm able to temper my mood.

Evelyn pulls her hand from mine and tries to get up but I place a hand across her thighs. "OK, I know. I'm sorry. I didn't mean it like that."

"For the record, *no*, I don't kiss my friends how I kiss you," she says. "But maybe I should."

I sober, glaring into her eyes.

Evelyn laughs. "I'm kidding."

"It's not funny," I say, lightening up. I relax on my elbows, lying back against the bed.

"No. It's not." She leans down on one arm to get closer. Evelyn surprises me when she smooths a hand through my hair, moving the curls off my forehead. "I like you." The confession is quiet, her voice barely a whisper.

I don't hesitate. Placing my arms around her waist, I hug her to me, lying down and pulling her soft warmth on top of my chest. "And I like you. A lot." Bringing her forehead to rest against mine, I kiss her again. I pour out all the feelings for her I've kept bottled up for so long. Feelings I've been hesitant to admit to for a while now. "Babe, you're beautiful," I whisper. "You see me. You don't enable me. You ... I feel comfortable with you. I want to let you in, tell you things I've never told anyone else. I want to be that for you too. I want you to tell me more about you, Ev. Your past, the things that ... I want—"

Evelyn hugs me, pulling me into a kiss that shakes me to the core, leaving no doubt she feels the same way I do. She's impatient with our embrace, tugging at my hands and placing them on herself.

"No, Ev." I stop her. "Have you been with anyone before?" I don't want to rush anything with her. She means more to me than that.

"No," she admits, cheeks flushing.

"Come here," I say, smiling. Her confession awakens some unknown emotion seeping its way into my chest. Framing her face, I bring her lips to mine.

We cuddle for a while, and when her cell phone goes off, I want to tell her not to get it, but I don't.

She lets go of me and retrieves her bag from the floor, pulling the phone out.

"Who is it?" I whisper, not wanting the moment to be over but inwardly dreading that it is.

"It's my dad. He's wondering when I'll be home."

And the moment's over.

"Yeah, we're done. Shepherd's bringing me home now," she says before hanging up. "Sorry. Can we head out?"

We still have time, and it's not like her dad's rushing her home, but I don't highlight that fact.

"Yeah, sure." I try to sound nonchalant like I'm not dejected that she's leaving so soon. I grab my keys from my desk. "You ready now?" I ask coolly, not meeting her gaze. I don't know why I'm annoyed, but I am.

I start walking to the door when she asks, "What's wrong? Did I do something?"

"No, you didn't. Let's go." I exit my room and head downstairs.

As soon as we're in my car, I'm backing out of the driveway. I don't say anything to her the whole way to her house, and she doesn't speak to me either.

"That shouldn't have happened, should it?" she asks when we pull up outside.

"Why shouldn't it have happened?" I ask, irritation present in my voice. "You're not with anyone, and neither am I."

"Well then, why do you look upset?"

"Did tonight mean anything?" I need to hear her tell me that it did. I'm needy, and it shocks the hell out of me. I'm never this clingy, but of course it's this way now. Everything with Evelyn is complicated.

"Of course it did, Shepherd. I care about you. You're the first guy I've kissed. I'll always treasure that."

"How do you feel about us?" I know I'm making myself vulnerable to her, but I don't care anymore.

"I'm comfortable. Like I said, I like you."

"This means more to me than comfort." I reach for her. I don't stop kissing her until she pulls gently at me.

"My parents," she whispers.

I release her. "Ev," I say, clearing my throat. "Will you go out with me?" When the words leave my lips, I realize how much I want her to be mine. How long I've been wanting it.

She hesitates, then looks at me. "Shepherd, I like you a lot," she confesses, "but I have to think about it. There're a lot of things you don't know about me. Things that, maybe when you find them out, might change how you feel now."

Not giving me a chance to respond to her cryptic statement, she places her lips against my cheek. "I'll see you tomorrow." She gets out of the car and walks up to her house.

I watch her go in.

Even though my gut keeps telling me something's off about what she said, I'm grinning like a clown because she said she'll think about it.

Chapter Sixteen

EVIE

By any means necessary.

I keep that thought trained in my mind because I refuse to let what happened with Shepherd shake me.

Even though it wasn't a part of the plan, it was necessary to get him to believe I felt something. He would believe anything I tell him right now.

He probably feels special he's the first guy I've kissed.

I told him I cared about him, but I had to. He practically begged for it.

I was surprised when he asked me to be his girlfriend. But I got over it, because it meant I won.

During our third-period class this morning, he couldn't take his eyes off me. Every time I glanced at him or happened to look in his direction, he was staring at me. I smiled at him a couple of times to reassure him I didn't have any regrets. He grinned in response and then tried to refocus his attention on the lecture.

I'm on my way to lunch with Tiffany. We're discussing our assignment for poetry next period, when Shepherd steps out in front of us, before we reach the cafeteria doors.

"Hey. Can I steal her for a sec?" He nods toward me, placing a hand on my forearm.

Tiffany looks at me, and I nod. "Sure," she replies, then walks ahead of us.

When she disappears through the double doors, Shepherd threads his fingers through mine and walks us over to an archway. We stand near the large floor-to-ceiling windows overlooking the school grounds below.

He leans down to kiss me, but I turn away. "Shepherd, no," I whisper, glancing around.

"I don't care who sees us," he says, grabbing me by the waist and pulling me into him. "We're not going to pretend, hiding in the bushes like a pair of teenagers doing something wrong."

I look up at him then.

"I've been waiting forever to hold you like this." He brings his lips near my ear and continues in a low whisper, "Did you think about it?"

I know he's talking about the prospect of us being together. Of course, there wasn't much to think about, all things considered. I'm quiet for a bit and he pulls me in even closer, his intense gaze daring me to refuse him.

"Yeah," I say.

"What?"

"Yes." I smile up at him. "I'll go out with you."

"Yaaasssss!" he groans out. This time when he bends his mouth to mine, I let him. But when after a few seconds, he starts getting carried away, I place my fingers between our lips.

"Shepherd," I warn.

"You're my girlfriend." He turns to glance at a few students passing by us, casting curious glances our way. "They'll all know you're mine sooner or later." He's so loud, I'm sure the whole school will know before we even enter the cafeteria. He takes my hand, interlacing our fingers again, and walks us to the doors.

I don't stop him.

This is a part of the initiation process, and I need him to willingly, without coaxing or persuasion on my part, make me a part of his life. The more embedded I become in every aspect of it, the more it'll hurt when I finally ruin his father.

I'm gonna make them hurt just as much as they hurt you.

Pain for pain.

We enter the cafeteria holding hands, and I feel several eyeballs tracking us to the lunch line, then over to the table where Shepherd usually sits with his friends.

The first person I notice when we get to his table is Beanca. She's shooting daggers at us, well, at me. My phone vibrates as soon as I sit down, but before I can reach for it I hear, "Whoa, dude. You gotta fill us in on what's going on."

Lucas is looking at us with eyebrows raised. He gestures between Shepherd and me as he continues. "You two have some explaining to do."

"Where's Jones?" Shepherd asks, directing the question at Beanca.

"I don't know. Am I his keeper?" she snaps, averting her gaze from everyone at the table.

"Someone's got a pole up her ass," Lucas comments. "Just answer the question, Bee. Where'd Jones go after bio? I'm curious myself because he seems to have made a habit out of not showing up for lunch these days."

"Listen, he didn't tell me where he was going. He just mentioned he'd see us later." Her bitchy attitude is already grating on me, and I try tuning her out. I take my phone out to check my message.

Tiffany: What the hell is going on between you and Shepherd?

Me: It's a long story. I'll fill you in later.

Tiffany: ???

Me: He asked me to be his gf.

Tiffany: What?!!! And you said yes?!

Me: lol Everyone deserves a chance, right?

Tiffany: Yeah, no. I'm gonna need to be "filled in" for sure.

I close the phone and look up to find Beanca smirking at me.

"What?" I ask.

"Oh nothing," she replies, sarcasm dripping from her words. "It's interesting how you ditched Jones and now you're with Shepherd. I'm wondering if Lucas is next. No judgment or anything, just curious."

"Beanca, don't," Shepherd says, glaring at her.

"For the record, I was never *with* Jones. We're friends, end of."

"Sure."

"No, not *sure*. She never slept with Jones, so stop trying to imply it." Shepherd stands, holding his tray in one hand as he reaches for my hand. "Let's go. I'm not letting her ruin your day."

"Ruin *my* day?" No. Beanca has less than 0 percent control over any aspect of my life.

"How do you think Chase is gonna feel when she finds out you've added another chick to your smorgasbord of conquests?" she asks, eyeing Shepherd and me in disgust.

I've had it. "Listen, if you have a problem with Shepherd dating me, then say it. But don't you dare call me anybody's conquest, because *nothing* could be further from the truth."

"Actually, you're right," she says, the smirk back on her face. "*You're* the real player here, jumping from one guy to the other like a game of hot potato. Must be nice having such an eclectic group of men desire you."

"Beanca, what the hell are you talking about?" Shepherd asks, narrowing his eyes at her. "You know what? No. You need to start getting used to having Evelyn around. Showing some respect is at the forefront of that. You got it?"

When Beanca remains silent, Lucas looks between Shepherd and her and then over at me. "Oh, that's what's going on here. Bee, you're jealous. This whole time I'm over here trying to figure out what the hell's crawled up your ass. I get it now."

"Lucas, I'm not jealous. Give me a break."

"Yes you are. Admit it. You can't stand the fact that Shepherd's actually calling someone his girlfriend. And that person isn't you."

Lucas rises several notches in my eyes saying this.

"Wow, you're *such* a jerk," Beanca says, her eyes filled with anger and some other emotion I can't decipher. "I can't even believe we're friends." She stands up, but before she can leave, Lucas clamps a hand on her forearm.

"Where're you going?" he demands.

"Nowhere," Beanca says in a choked voice. She pulls her arm from Lucas's grasp with such force that some of the food on her tray flops onto the table, the floor, and the sleeve of his jacket. Of course, she doesn't apologize. Instead, she stalks off like a petulant child.

Lucas picks up one of the napkins from off the table to wipe his sleeve. "She'll get over it. I don't think she's ever really had to share any of our devotion to her." He says this all while cleaning his jacket, not looking at us. When he finally looks up, we both sit down. "Shepherd's messed around with other girls, but she never felt threatened unless she thought it might get serious. Now that he's with you, and has given you an official title, her fight response is on high."

The way he's able to analyze Beanca's whole demeanor has me looking at him in awe. Seriously, the guy is a lot smarter than I ever gave him credit for.

Shepherd suddenly leans over and kisses the corner of my mouth. "You're staring, babe. Should I be worried?" he whispers playfully in my ear, before pulling my chair closer until it's flush against his. He places a palm on my thigh, squeezing it.

"Shepherd, people can see us," I say quietly.

"Let 'em. I'm never letting you go," he whispers.

I try to remain unaffected by his words, but my face feels warm and my stomach flutters.

Chapter Seventeen

SHEPHERD

Evelyn is my girlfriend.

I didn't think she would ever be into me. I mean, I know I'm attractive, but my hang-up was that I thought she'd go for guys more like Jones.

I've been trying to get her to open up to me more, let me in on her life and everything about her. It hasn't been easy. As a matter of fact, it's bordered on impossible.

She already met my dad and Jackie, while I'd only met her dad. I wanted to meet her mom, so I suggested that I go to her place for one of our sessions instead. At first she seemed reluctant, but I insisted.

Evelyn has a strong relationship with both of her parents. I'm happy for her. I only wish she could open up to me about other stuff. There's a sadness behind her eyes sometimes, and she tries to mask it, but I know it's there. When I ask her about anything in her past, she cages up. I'm so determined to find out, I persuaded her parents to let the sessions be at their place from now on. This way it saves both them and me a trip.

When asked about that, about Evelyn not having a car, her mom said it was her choice not theirs. Of course, she didn't explain why that is. All she said was that she does fine without one.

What teenager has the chance to get a car and turns it down?

She's such an enigma. But I'm not giving up until I peel away all her layers.

"I got us something on the way here," I say.

Evelyn opens her front door a little wider for me to pass. I walk in with the food I'd ordered and picked up.

"What is it?" She eyes the bags, then closes the door and follows me. "You know you didn't have to. I could've made something for us."

"You know what?" I grin, placing the paper bags on the table. "I would've preferred that." I take the containers of food out and place them on the table. I look over at her, and when I do, I immediately sober up.

"What is it?" I ask, confused at her sudden discomfort.

"Shepherd." She grows rigid. "Thanks for going through all the trouble but ... I don't eat sushi."

"That's OK," I say. "There's a first time for everything."

"I didn't say I never *tried* sushi, just that I don't eat it. As in I don't like it."

"Ev, there are so many different kinds. Are you telling me you've tried them *all* and still didn't find at least one you liked?"

She doesn't answer me but walks over to the living room to grab her backpack.

Great, now I've upset her.

Deciding not to press the issue, I start opening the containers. I bought three different rolls.

When she gets back and sees the spread, she ignores it and proceeds to prepare for the session. "Can we start?"

"Which one didn't you like?" I must be a glutton for punishment.

"Is it so hard to believe that I might just not like sushi because I just *don't* like it?"

"Tell me which one you don't like, and I'll leave it alone."

She's quiet.

I grab one of the veggie rolls with a pair of chopsticks and bending to her, I attempt to bring it to her mouth.

"What are you doing?" she asks, pushing my hand away.

I pop that piece into my mouth and grab the smoked salmon next. I try to bring that to her mouth and she does the same thing. I pop that in my mouth too. When I try to bring the California to her mouth next, she slaps the shit out of my hand. She stands up so sharply the chair screeches against the floor.

"I don't want to try the damned sushi, Shepherd! Just respect that already!" Her breathing is sporadic as she stands looking at me, face torrid.

That's when I realize this isn't about sushi. This isn't about whether she likes it or not. Hell it's not even about me trying to get her to try it. There's something deeper, something I've touched that she wants to keep buried.

And damn, I want to dig it up.

"I'm sorry," she says, working to conceal her emotions from me. "I—let's just start OK." She sits back down and scoots her chair in.

Not happening.

"What happened to you?" I ask, refusing to let her crawl back into the shell she's constructed around herself.

She furrows her brows, looking as if she's about to deny it.

I stop her. "Don't tell me it's nothing. Did someone do something to you? Hurt you in some way?"

"This is ridiculous." She chooses one of the sushi rolls and pops it into her mouth, barely chewing it before swallowing. "Satisfied?" she asks, looking up at me in frustration.

I don't reply.

She reaches for another one and does the same thing. When I'm still silent, she reaches for another one, then another one, until she's almost choking.

Reaching my arms out, I stop her and pull her up against me. She fights me, but I hold her in my arms. I rub my palm against her back.

She stops struggling against me.

Deciding not to push any further, I make a mental note to ask her parents about the sushi.

"I care about you, baby. I want—" I don't get to finish because Evelyn brings her mouth up to cover mine.

She starts slanting her lips, dragging her mouth across mine and trying to get me to open up. When I do, she instantly delves into my mouth.

I want to enjoy the kiss, but I know she's using it to shut me up. I hit a sensitive spot she doesn't want touched, and she's trying to distract me. When she moves her hand against me, I stop her.

"Please," she whispers against my lips before kissing me again.

If all I wanted from Evelyn was a physical relationship, I would give in. Her wanting me is a given. She wants me physically inside her. My goal is to be mentally inside her, to figure her out, to tap the emotional depth that makes her who she is.

When she starts tugging me toward the stairs, I resist. "What are you trying to do?"

"I want to show you how much I care about you."

"Ev, let's get some studying done."

She looks over at the books and containers of sushi and drags her eyes back to mine. "You'd rather do that?"

"Don't say it like that. You know it's not like that."

"Fine, whatever." She drops her hands and goes over to collect her stuff from the table.

"Where're you going?"

"The living room. I don't feel like studying in here. And you can't bring your food because my mom will skin us both if anything gets on her carpet." She leaves me standing there, the containers lying open on the table, all of which she'd just eaten from.

The same sushi she says she doesn't like.

The same sushi she claims she doesn't eat.

There're a lot of things you don't know about me, Shepherd, things that maybe when you find them out, might change how you feel now.

Yeah, I've got my work cut out for me, but hell if I'm not up for the challenge.

Chapter Eighteen

EVIE

Regret.

It consumes me.

I hit my chest repeatedly, remembering how I betrayed Ethan's memory. After his death, I swore I would never touch the things he loved.

He loved sushi.

We fought over it the night he died.

It was like a pact I'd made with him in a way. I never ate it with him when he was alive, so I wouldn't touch it in his absence. I broke that promise. I hadn't just touched it or simply eaten it. I'd stuffed my mouth with it. All because Shepherd wouldn't stop. He keeps prying and prying.

The other day, when he came over, he wanted to check out my room. My dad was home, so I had an excuse to deny him entrance. I had keepsakes and photographs of my brother in my bedroom, so I stowed them away in case he decides to snoop around.

I'm trying to speed up the process with phase two. If not, he might catch on to something, and then all this would have been for nothing.

Shepherd's almost been an open book with me. I guess he's doing it in hopes I'll return the favor. He's shared stories with me about his childhood in that huge house. He told me a big house didn't mean a family with as big a heart. Instead of warmth, he'd felt left behind, didn't feel like he'd been anybody's priority. His dad had taken on a string of women, and not all had had good intentions where Shepherd was concerned. He didn't go into detail, and I didn't push him either. I had no leg to stand on because I wasn't forthcoming myself.

His dad being a serial cheater definitely didn't come as a shock. I mean, it was typical for a man like him. Hadn't he used manipulative tactics to avoid any real punishment for his crime? Or crimes ...

Who knows?

He's probably cheated the system as many times as he's cheated the women, and his son out of knowing the value he held in the eyes of a loving parent.

I have no doubt that Shepherd's mom was a victim of circumstance. He doesn't want to see it, because she left. He was too young at the time, and as kids we only see the value in people who actually give us the time and attention we crave. Even though I don't think he found that in his father, he was the parent who was there. So even if his mom has a valid excuse for having gotten the hell out of that house, he wouldn't have known anything about it.

Physical presence didn't automatically equal being present in a child's life though. And even though I can see evidence of his father trying now, it almost seems like he does that for outward appearances, not out of any real depth of feeling for his son. I don't have to be a rocket scientist to see the only attention Shepherd gets is that of making sure he's doing what he's supposed to do to keep up appearances. His family name and political ties require it of him. Shepherd plays the dutiful son role to a tee. And I wonder if it's out of habit or because he's desperate for his father's approval?

Either way, Mr. Buchanan's dutiful son is fast becoming my dutiful lover. Like he'd taken my brother from me, taken my parents' only son from them, I would see to it he lost his precious little heir too.

He's practically handed Shepherd to me. I shower him with affection he didn't get from the mom who left, affection he doesn't get from daddy *not-so-dearest*.

I'm just waiting to hear those three words.

Those three precious words uttered from his heart are the only green light I need.

I'm so close I can almost *taste* the victory.

I have one last plan that, if done just right, will solidify my place in his heart. I wasn't only Helen of Troy. I was the Trojan horse that would be embedded in that secret chamber. If anyone touched me, tried to set me on fire, I wouldn't be the only one burned.

Shepherd told me his parents are out of town for the weekend, so we're hanging at his place. We plan to go do some indoor rock climbing and then order in. I told my parents I was hanging out at Tiffany's place for the night. Shepherd has practice, so I recruited Tiffany to help me set up a small tent in his backyard.

"I still can't believe you two are *actually* together," she says as she places the tent poles through on her side. "Shepherd's never gone steady before. I mean, there was that one girl from freshman year, but that didn't last long."

"Girl from freshman year?" I ask. Shepherd told me he's never had a girlfriend before.

"Yeah, but they were together for like less than a month before he left her high and dry." She starts getting another pole ready to complete the tent frame.

"Why?" I fumble while getting a peg to hammer into place. It shouldn't bother me who Shepherd dated in the past, so I don't know why I feel lied to.

"People said she'd either lied about something major or cheated on him, one of the two. Either way, she was a mess. She ended up leaving our school, moved to some other state."

The story causes goose bumps to crawl across my skin. I tuck my jacket closer around me.

I place two sleeping bags in the tent along with a few warm blankets. We set up the portable fire pit next, placing two lawn chairs next to it.

"This is so cute." Tiffany stands next to me, looking at the finished product. "All you need now are speakers, you know, music to set the mood."

"Right over here." I go over to my duffle bag and fish the portable speakers out, placing them on the tiny table we'd put between the chairs. Our task complete, we head back into the house.

Tiffany and I pass some time talking about what's going on between her and Casey. She's been hanging with him a lot lately and not saying much about their status.

"We're just friends."

"Is that how you want it to stay? I remember Jones saying Casey's interested."

"I don't know. It's like I hear you say that, and Jones hints at it, but Casey hasn't *said* anything to me yet. All he does is get all prickly when I hang out with other guys but does *nothing* about it. It's not like I try to make him jealous, but I can tell he's annoyed and doesn't say anything." She sighs in frustration.

We talk about it some more and I suggest she ask him in a subtle way what his feelings are. Sometimes maneuvering these situations can be tricky, but I advise to let her instincts tell her how exactly to go about it.

She leaves, and I head to Shepherd's room. I shower and change into a baby-pink off-the-shoulder top and white denim. I do my makeup and then throw my twists over one shoulder as they fall to my waist.

Before I leave his room, I give myself a once-over in the colossal hallway mirror, then head downstairs. I shouldn't, but I head to his dad's office.

When I try the knob, it doesn't budge.

"Damn it."

I should have known he would've locked it.

I get a chair to try and search above the door but find nothing. I do the same for the bathroom door across the hall, but still no luck.

Where could he have hidden it?

When an idea comes to me, I tell myself there's no way he would have put it in such an obvious place. But I go there anyway. I open the front door, and instead of checking the flower box on the right windowsill, I check the one on the left.

Bingo.

I take the golden key to the office door and sure enough it clicks. Pushing the door open, I enter the room.

I decide to try the desk first. I'm looking for anything that even remotely mentions Shepherd's biological mother.

I search through the drawers but find nothing. My hands land on the bottom right drawer. It's locked. I try to pull at it again, and when I inspect it, I find a keyhole. Which means I won't be getting into it that easily. I don't have a bobby pin so I look around the room for anything I can use.

When I spot a metal letter opener, I try that.

Nothing.

I take a paper clip from a container on the office desk, and try that too.

Still nothing.

I'm about to give up, when I get an inkling to check underneath the surface of the desk itself.

When I do, I feel a small key dangling from a hook.

Are you serious?

I waste no time.

Once I'm in, I start sifting through different paperwork and documentation. I see a deed to the house and I keep searching. I find an explicit image of one, no wait, two ... are you freaking kidding me? There're a stack of images of women in the most degrading of positions. Some are tied up, some with gags, some with bruises, others with both.

I'm so disgusted I almost slam the drawer closed. But then my hand lands against a cold metal case. I immediately grab hold of it and pull it out.

When I open it, I notice a lock of blond hair in a baggie. I move that aside to see an image of Shepherd as a toddler in his mother's arms. He couldn't be more than two years old in the picture. His tiny hand is wrapped around her index finger and she's kissing his cheek. Below that image, there are about five more with him and her. The last one he's actually in uniform as he holds on to her leg. He's crying in the photo so I assume it must have been taken on his very first day of school. I place the photos back into the case and as I'm about to close it, my eyes catch on a small red piece of paper. I wouldn't have noticed it had it not been for the color.

It's dated about nine years ago ... the same year as my brother's accident.

I want to see my son. Don't you think you've kept him from me long enough?
If you don't let me see him, I'll tell—

The rest of the paper is torn away. When I flip it around to see if there's anything on the back, it's blank.

What the hell?

So she hadn't abandoned him.

The front door opens, and my heart all but leaps into my throat. I drop the note back into the case and close it.

"Evelyn," Shepherd calls out.

I try to stay quiet as my fingers work to place the case in the exact position it had been in. I fix the documents and stack of images back over it and glide the drawer closed. I faintly hear Shepherd's movement on the stairs.

I turn the lock and replace the key on its hook under the desk, then go through the office door and lock that too. When I get to the front door, Shepherd is on his way back downstairs and spots me. I immediately pocket the key to the office.

"Babe, you didn't answer my texts." He walks over and kisses me. "Then I saw your things in my room but you weren't there. You didn't hear me calling for you?"

"Your house is huge, babe," I reply, evading his question. "Come here." I grab hold of his wrist and take him toward the back porch. "I have a surprise for you."

"What is it?"

I open the back door and release him, stepping aside. I look at his face, wanting to gauge his reaction.

Shepherd's gaze falls on the tent, the fire pit, and the chairs. They're in a small area of his backyard. His face takes on the boyish charm I've become familiar with. The wind blows his blond curls ever so slightly over his forehead.

Something in my chest flutters suddenly. I frown, placing a flattened palm against my heart.

"Why'd you do all this?" Shepherd asks, turning to me.

I look up then to find his expression sober.

"I want to make good memories for you here," I say softly.

He thinks for a second and then says, "Ev, I don't want your pity. I don't need you feeling sorry for me."

"What makes you think I did this out of pity?" I'm taken aback that he would take offense at this. "I just wanted to do something nice for you."

"Why this?"

I don't want to argue about this because that's *not* how I want this evening to go down. I choose my next few words with caution. "Because you're my boyfriend. Because I like spending time with you. I care about you." I move closer to him and place my palms on his chest.

He searches my face, then puts his arms around my waist, holding me against him. "I'm sorry." He lowers his head to mine, placing a gentle kiss on my forehead.

"Do you like it?"

"Yeah, it's pretty cool." He looks over at the setup. "Did you do all this by yourself?"

"No, Tiffany helped me out. She left a couple hours ago."

When he turns to walk us toward the tent, I stop him.

"We don't get to camp out until after we get back." I tug at him to walk us back into the house instead.

"Is that so?" He glides his hand to the seat of my jeans and smacks me. "I'm looking forward to it then."

Chapter Nineteen

EVIE

I enjoy indoor rock climbing.

I would enjoy it even more if Shepherd wasn't being a jerk to the instructor. I'm not acting that way with the girls who've been vying for his attention.

"Shepherd, that was *rude*."

He shoulders his way between me and the guy who's trying to give me pointers for one of the more challenging climbs. "He's basically offering to carry you on his back," he whispers. He moves us away, creating a wide gap between the instructor and me.

"Shepherd, stop it." I step around him as soon as he releases me and gesture for the instructor to continue.

Following the guy's directions, I place my hands and feet on the first couple of handholds. When I'm unsure of where to put my foot, the instructor grabs hold of my ankle, guiding my leg up to one of the farther footholds. I almost slip, but he steadies me with a hand on my calf.

I keep climbing. But when it becomes impossible, the

instructor comes up after me. When he gets close enough, he starts giving me pointers on what to do next. Twice, he takes hold of my hand, and once, he places his hand on my back, preventing me from failing the climb. When I finally hit the buzzer at the top, I'm exhilarated.

"You did pretty good," he compliments once we're back down. "A lot of people give up when the wall protrudes like that, but you were up for the challenge. Very impressive."

"Thanks." We shake hands and I turn away. I'm feeling awesome. I search the area to see where Shepherd's gone off to.

A few moments later, I spot him talking to the same girl who'd been trying to flirt with him earlier. He bends to look at something she's showing him on her phone. His eyes flicker upward as he catches sight of me walking toward them.

"Hey," I say when I finally get to them.

The girl looks up, then over at Shepherd.

He doesn't acknowledge me but keeps his gaze intent on her phone.

I'm so annoyed at his level of immaturity that I stalk over to another one of the difficult climbs. After a while, I chance a look to find him walking over to another wall with the same girl.

He's trying to piss me off and being petty over a guy who was just doing his job.

About half an hour later, we get in his car and leave the rock climbing center. We drive back in total silence.

Out of the two of us, I was the only one who had the actual right to be upset. He deliberately ignored me for the last half of our date and allowed some girl to flirt with him in front of me. I hate it when guys act immature. I wanted our weekend to be perfect, but he'd already managed to sour it—from getting testy with me about the camping setup in his backyard to being a complete jerk to me during our date.

I have every intention of either going home or to Tiffany's place, where I'd already lied and told my parents I'd be anyway.

When Shepherd opens the front door, I head straight up to his room to get my things. I throw my duffel over my shoulder, descend the stairs and open the door. I'll go stand out on the curb and call Tiffany to come get me. It's dark out, but I don't care.

"Where the hell are you going?" Shepherd clamps down on my arm as I try to make my exit.

"I'm going home." I yank my arm free and continue out the door.

He comes after me. Wrapping both arms around me from behind, he lifts me up and carries me back into the house.

I struggle against him, the duffle falling in the process.

He drops me on one of the sofas in the living room, then stands towering over me. His face is flushed, his features rigid. Not saying anything, he continues standing there staring at me.

I try to get up off the couch.

His hands fly out and he grabs hold of my upper arms.

"*Ow*, Shepherd, that hurts." His hands are like a vise around my upper arms.

He immediately releases me, and I rub my arms.

"My dad's been cheating on Jackie since before they got married," he says out of nowhere. He's not looking at me now. "He's had many women come in and out of our house. Some of them were normal. Others were ... sick," he continues.

I listen, not sure why he's choosing to tell me all this

now. A part of me is seething from his behavior tonight, but the other part is curious about what he has to say.

"There was one woman, Rachael. I liked her, thought she was super pretty. She was engaged to my dad. Anyway, something happened between them and she came to my room crying one night. I was fourteen at the time, and she told me I was the only one who actually cared about her. Then, she kissed me."

I gasp, bringing my hand to my mouth, taken aback by the confession.

Shepherd glances at me but continues talking. He sits, and I do too, careful to give him some space. Not liking that, he closes the gap between us, placing a hand over my thigh.

"At first, I hesitated because she was my dad's fiancé. But then she kissed me again and started touching me. I was a teenager with no experience, so I felt things for the first time. Things I liked feeling. One thing led to another, and before I realized it, we were sleeping together.

My mouth falls open out of disgust for the woman's actions.

"My dad walked in on us that night in bed together. He dragged her out of my room and the two of them started arguing. I thought she cared about me. But then she started saying these vile things to him. She said she'd used me, like my dad had used her, and her mother. Said we deserved whatever was coming to us. Then she told him I'd end up like him, abandoned by the one person he loved.

"She told my dad that my mother had taken on lovers because he hadn't been able to satisfy her. That she'd found a man who was strapped enough, and left both me and my dad because we didn't *do it* for her anymore."

As his past unfolds, something inside me cracks, dissolving into tiny pieces, before dissipating altogether. A soft substance replaces it, flowing outward from nonexistent walls.

"After that day," he continues, "the day Rachael left, nothing was the same. Dad couldn't forget what happened, and neither could I. Our relationship was never the same."

I don't know what to say when he finishes. I look at my hands where they rest in my lap, and move them over to cover his, where it tightens around my thigh.

"Evelyn, I get possessive sometimes. I've noticed it's an automatic behavior I have with you. Even if you're not going to, my brain's running message is that you'll lie to me, cheat on me, or abandon me when you find someone else better."

When he says this, my mind runs to what Tiffany told me earlier today. Shepherd dated some girl their freshman year. He'd broken up with her in less than a month because she'd lied to him.

An odd sensation fills my chest again, a kind of fraying away at my nerves. Letting go of his hands, I stand up, inhaling deeply and hoping the feeling will go away. I face away from Shepherd, telling myself it's because I don't want him thinking I'm pitying him.

His arms come around me and he bends his head, bringing it to rest against the side of my face.

"Baby, I keep messing up with you," he says, disappointment in his voice. "I'm trying to fix it, fix me."

I relax back into him.

Every word he's uttered reaches deep into me, and I want him closer.

I turn in his arms, my heart in my throat. "Me too." I whisper the words, my voice shaky. I reach up on my toes and brush my lips against his.

Shepherd lifts me into his arms, moving frantic lips over

mine. He grabs one of the huge throws off the couch and heads toward the back door.

I know we're outside when I feel the cool breeze against my skin.

He's still kissing me when we get to the tent. He opens the flap, places me down, then spreads the throw on the tent floor. When he notices the blankets in one corner, he looks over at me.

"Come here," he says, reaching for me. We snuggle comfortably under one of the warm fluffy blankets.

I lie against his chest for a while, enjoying the feel of him.

"I love you, Ev." Shepherd trails soft kisses from my forehead, down to my nose, and then across my mouth. "Do you think you'll ever want kids when you get older?" he asks.

"Yeah, but we're still in high school and I'm still a child myself. We have our whole lives ahead of us. Graduation, college ..." I trail off absentmindedly, making circles on his shoulder with my fingers.

He's quiet for a moment.

"That's what you're waiting for, isn't it?" His voice is somber.

My gaze shifts to his, and when I see that he's upset I turn and slightly push up from his chest.

"That's what you want," he continues. "To go off to college and meet other guys." He avoids looking at me as he too sits up, subsequently causing my arms to fall away from him.

"Don't say stuff like that when you know it's not true." I frown in confusion, wondering at the turn in the conversation.

"Isn't it? When we graduate were you planning on marrying me, Evelyn?"

My mouth damn near hits the floor of the tent. "What are you talking about, Shepherd? We never said anything about getting *married*."

"I knew it," he says, shaking his head.

"Knew what?"

"This is just some high school fling for you, isn't it?"

"I don't think that at all."

"So then tell me, Ev. Would you marry me if I asked you to?"

I open my mouth to say no, but the vengeful part says ...

By any means necessary.

This was a part of the plan wasn't it? Getting him completely wrapped up in *us*? I find myself in a struggle against my own thoughts.

"Of course I would, but we're still too young to decide that," I finally reply.

"I love *you*, and I want to be with *you*. I don't think age factors in here."

I don't want to ruin the moment so I kiss him in a way that shows how much I only love *him* and want to be with *him* too. "And I love you. Now can we get something to eat? I'm starving." I chuckle to lighten the mood, rub my nose against his, then exit the tent.

I walk ahead of him, telling myself that I told him I loved him because it was a part of the plan. Shepherd admitted that he loves me, and I only repeated those words back to him out of necessity.

I didn't mean them. I couldn't mean them.

Chapter Twenty

SHEPHERD

I don't know what Evelyn has done to me, but she's made me want things, need things, I never even thought of having.

When I'd asked her if she'd marry me if I asked, I wanted to smack the hell out of my mouth for asking such a vibe kill of a question. Who wants to get married when they haven't even gotten a chance to be free from the shackles of boring-ass academia?

We aren't even eighteen yet. I got way ahead of myself. I need to get a handle on how much of this neediness I allow to show because I've been doing a real shitty job of it so far.

But the thing is, I can't see myself with anyone else now.

She's the one I want.

I love her feistiness, her passion, how much she doesn't put up with my crap, and how comfortable I am with fully being myself around her.

I revealed so much to her this past weekend, and she'd listened to me, didn't try to pander to me, didn't pity me.

And when she'd admitted to also having a brokenness that needed fixing, our connection felt raw, real. It was the closest she'd come to revealing her past to me, the sadness present in her eyes, that I'd seen a few times.

"Shep, have you seen Beanca?" Lucas asks, interrupting my thoughts. He enters the locker room, a worried look on his face. "I asked Jones and he said she wasn't in class today, and she wasn't at lunch either."

"Maybe she isn't here today. Text her," I tell him.

"I did, *and* I called her. She's been screening my calls."

"Did you guys get into another fight?"

Lucas looks at me, exasperated.

They've been doing that a lot lately. Fighting over some of *the* most asinine shit. What's strange is that Beanca's usually the one breaking up fights, not being a part of them. Recently she and Lucas have taken it up a notch, going at it like chihuahuas who've discovered they have to share the same space.

"She's probably upset with me for the same reason she's upset with you," he suggests as he opens his locker and takes out his duffle, replacing it with his book bag.

"Uh ... what're you talking about?" I ask.

"Dude, Beanca is territorial. When you started dating Evelyn, the claws came out."

I frown.

He had a point there. Beanca hasn't left it a mystery how she felt about Evelyn and me being together. She was also hostile toward her when she thought Jones might start dating her.

"After homecoming, I've gone on a couple dates with Michelle," Lucas continues. "Now Beanca's giving me the cold shoulder."

Michelle is one of the members of the band he's a part of. I've seen her a couple of times. She's alright.

"Didn't you say she'll get over stuff like this?" I ask, throwing his own words back at him. "Give her some time. I'm sure she didn't expect it to be only the four of us forever. When she finds some guy she cares about, you'll see how much she'll change her tune."

Lucas's jaw tightens, and he looks away. "Still, it makes me angry when she does this."

"Huh?" I can't hear his mumbling because a few of the others enter, and they're yelling across at each other as they start changing for practice.

"When she cuts us off," he continues, "she shuts down and goes all cold and that shit is *not* cool," he says in frustration.

I don't think Lucas realizes how much he's letting Beanca's mood swings affect him. If I didn't know any better, I'd say he's interested. But I know Lucas. He values their friendship too much to date Beanca. For him, crossing the line from a platonic to a romantic relationship would be irreversible. And if it didn't work out, it would ruin the years-long friendship they've worked hard to safeguard.

That's his problem. Sometimes, Lucas can be too analytical to enjoy the spontaneity of life.

"Like I said. Give her time." I continue getting ready for practice.

Lucas strides to his locker, his shoulders slumped.

He isn't the only one on someone's no-call list. Jones hasn't been speaking to me much lately either. I know why but our situation was impossible. I was interested in Evelyn as much as he was at the time he'd announced it to us. I'd been in denial about it. She wasn't into him though.

I'm giving him time to come around. And although it

seems it's taking a bit longer than expected, I don't think his present distraction has anything to do with Evelyn. No, Jones not showing up at lunch seems a lot more calculated than that. I actually think he's got some hang-up some-where. He's got to have a girl he's trying to keep on the low. When he used to take Evelyn and Tiffany to lunch, he did the same thing. He wouldn't show up to eat with us but chose to spend that time in the presence of the girl he was interested in. That's the case now. And he's likely using me going out with Evelyn as his cover for ditching us.

Of course what I'm thinking could be complete bullshit. But I know Jones. He can be petty.

So what gives Jones?

I look over at him, where he's currently talking to Dudley about something. The two head out to the field.

A few of us finish up and follow them out.

I'm leaving football practice, my bag over my shoulder, when I get a text.

I reach into my pocket and pull out my phone, pausing to look at the message on the way to my car. It's from some number I don't know and I'm about to pocket it, but I see that it's a video. Thinking it's one of the players on the team sending out a mass text, I hit play.

The moment the video starts, I narrow my eyes.

I immediately notice my dad's office. He's leaning on the edge of his desk looking over at someone he's speaking with. I can only see his left profile.

I start wondering what the hell I'm watching when the other person comes into view. I bring the phone closer as I recognize who my dad's talking to.

Evelyn?

What is this?

She approaches my dad, and the outfit she's wearing is completely inappropriate. Her skirt is so short I can almost see her underwear, and her top leaves nothing to the imagination. She walks toward my dad, moving in a way that almost makes me think she's—

I suppress the thought but continue watching.

She says something to him, then brings her mouth up to his, slanting her lips across his. She reaches her arms around his neck and—

I instantly look away from the screen.

I feel heat rise to my head and neck. My chest ceases up, and I think I'm going to be sick.

I don't know how long I'm standing there. My chest keeps rising and falling, and it's like I can't catch my breath fast enough.

Then I'm moving.

I eat up the distance between me and my car and barely close the door before I'm ripping out of the student parking lot.

I don't even see the other cars as I speed through traffic. I need to see her. I need to talk to her. I need to know what the hell is going on.

I need ...

I feel physically ill, so I find a place to pull over and jump out of my car. I gulp in large breaths of air and try to exhale but end up coughing out instead.

A few minutes later, I get back in my car, but my head is still going crazy, one thought barely ending before another one begins.

Distracted, I finally register the car horn coming from behind me. I realize the light has changed and I've been holding up the lane. I speed off, anger building up inside me the closer I get to her place.

I try to calm down, but as soon as I get there I'm out of my car within seconds and pounding on her door. When Evelyn doesn't open it fast enough, I almost lose it. I pull my phone out of my pocket so fast it falls.

"Damn it!"

When I reach down to pick it up and go to call Evelyn, her front door opens.

"Hey, babe," she says, smiling. Her smile falters when she sees my face. "Why do you look so upset? What's wrong?"

"That's what I'd like to know," I groan out as I step around her and into the house. "Are you alone?"

"Yeah ... my parents are getting in late today," she replies, looking at me, worry creasing her brow.

Good.

We have the house to ourselves.

I step into the living room, and without preamble, I scroll to the message and thrust my phone at her.

She looks at it confused, then takes it from me.

I tell her to hit play and watch her reaction. "Is that you in the video?" I ask impatiently as she takes in what she's seeing.

She slowly looks up at me. I get my answer and I cover my mouth, looking everywhere but at her. It's not that I doubt that it's her in that video; I just need to have her admit it.

I start taking these deep-ass breaths, but it's like the more air I try to get into my lungs, the tighter they constrict.

"Evelyn, I swear," I say out loud. My voice is weak as hell and I get choked up. I'm *not* going to cry over this.

When she still doesn't say anything, I use my anger to keep myself from breaking down in front of her.

To hell with that.

She did this. And I'm not giving her the satisfaction of my damned tears.

"Are you not going to answer me? Is that you in the fu— in the video?" I'm trying not to cuss at her, but right now my self-control is hanging on like a rubber band that's about to bust.

"Where—where'd you get this?" she asks, looking down at the video, her eyes blinking rapidly. I can see panic there as they widen in disbelief.

I'm so crazed right now, I snatch the phone from her grasp and force her to look up at me. I must look deranged, because she flinches before stepping away from me.

The moment of fear is quickly concealed. Evelyn being who she is straightens her spine and says, "It's not what it looks like." Her false bravado is betrayed by the unsteadiness of her voice.

"Then explain. Explain to me why you and my dad—" I can't finish because the thought of it puts the images back in my head, making me want to hit something.

"Shepherd, I said it's not like that OK?"

"You said that. What I don't hear is you telling me what the hell it *is* like."

"Stop talking to me like that," she says, shaking her head and covering her face with her hands. She takes a breath, then looks up at me. "Look, you're angry right now—"

"You think?" I say, interrupting her for stating the obvious.

"And ... I just feel ... like we should talk about this when you're in a better head space and are willing to hear me out." She looks at me hesitantly. This is the first time since seeing that video that she allows her vulnerability to show. And I guess she thinks that'll get me to let up, because she reaches out a hand to touch me.

I instantly brush her hand away.

She pulls it back like I burned her.

"What makes you think you get to decide that?" Cocking my head to the side, I scowl at her, feeling my rage like a vise, closing in on every pore.

She flinches at my question but still says nothing.

Rubber band, meet bust.

"What happened after the video ended, *E-vie?* Huh? Did you two fu—?"

"Don't even say something disgusting like that!" she hisses at me before turning away, her hands fisted at her sides. She walks deeper into the living room in an attempt to distance herself from me. "I would *never* do that."

"Wouldn't you though? Maybe you have some sort of older dude fetish," I say, not giving a damn. As I utter the words, memories of my dad finding her in his office, the strange way she acted the night she helped me with my history paper, and the other times she's acted weird whenever she was over at my place come rushing back.

Like a bomb, my mind explodes and goes into overdrive coming up with its own theory since she's given me nothing.

I get sick to my stomach at the thought that she's only with me because she has a thing for my dad.

Just like Rachael ...

Rachael used me, maybe she was using me too.

Whirling from that theory, my eyes bug out and for the second time, I look away from her. I fight to keep the lead weight from pulverizing my chest.

"*No,* I wouldn't! You know me, Shepherd. You know I wouldn't do something like that!" she shouts.

"I *don't* know you!" I yell back, facing her again. "I thought I did, but the girl in that video ... the girl who could ... *do* that crap—"

"I used you OK! I used you," she admits, her breath hitching.

My eyes flicker as I try to process what the hell she just said to me. It's one thing to think it was possible for Evelyn to use me, it's another to hear her admit to it. I turn away from her and close my eyes, fighting to keep my breathing steady. The uncomfortable sensation in my chest flares and heats, burning its way throughout my entire body. I bring both my hands down the sides of my face and steeple them at my mouth, raising my gaze to the ceiling.

"You're dad he—he needs to pay for what he did," she says from behind me. "Instead, he gets to live, while my ..."

I have no idea what she's saying, and my forehead creases as I swing back around to face her.

"Shepherd, it was before us—before we got together." She gestures between us, a pained expression on her face. Her eyes glisten as unshed tears threaten to spill over.

I've never seen Evelyn cry.

Ever.

At the sight of the tears falling down her face ...

"I'm sorry," I hear her whisper on a shaky breath.

Hearing her apology makes everything all the more real. It doesn't matter when it happened. That's my dad, and no matter how hard I try, I can't *unsee* them in that office together, her kissing him, his hands on her.

The feeling of moisture hitting my cheek surprises me, and I squeeze my eyes shut to stop the flow. I *refuse* to break down over someone who didn't give a damn about me from the beginning.

Suddenly, the energy in the room shifts, and I feel,

rather than see Evelyn as she comes over to me. She closes her arms tightly around my waist, placing her head on my chest.

I let her.

I don't register what she's doing until her lips are on my neck, on my jaw. Her repeated whispers of "*I'm sorry*" echo in my ears as she raises on tiptoes to place soft kisses on my cheeks.

Again I let her.

But when her mouth brushes against mine in the same way she'd done to my dad in that video, the images play across my mind, and I immediately turn my head away.

When she still doesn't make a move to let me go, I reach my hands behind my back, grabbing hold of hers. I peel her arms from around me and shove them away.

"I can't. I can't even look at you," I say as I look around the room. "I'm outta here."

"Babe, please—" She attempts to prevent me from leaving by holding on to my upper arm.

"*Don't*," I say as I turn back to face her. I immediately steel myself against the hurt that flickers across her eyes. "*Don't* call me that."

Her mouth falls open as she continues staring at me.

"And don't *say* anything else because there's nothing you can say to take this back. I'm done with you." Not giving her a backward glance, I turn and stride out of the house, leaving her standing there.

As soon as I get in my car, I back out of the driveway so fast I almost hit a tree.

I'm angry.

I head straight to my dad's, which is probably not the best idea considering the shitty mood I'm in, but who gives a shit.

I park outside of his building, and it's like someone takes a blowtorch to my temper. Walking straight into his office, I ignore his secretary as she yells something to the effect of him being on some conference call.

I don't give a damn.

"I need to talk to you," I say as soon as I get in his office.

"Shep, I'm on a call. It'll have to wait."

"Can prison wait, too?" I probably look as insane as I feel, because he tells whoever is on the other line that something urgent's come up.

As soon as he puts the receiver down, I shove my cell phone in his face.

"What is this?" he asks, looking at the phone, then up at me.

"I don't know, Dad. Maybe you should watch it, then *you* can tell me."

I watch him as he hits play and takes in the contents of the video. When his eyes widen and he brings his free hand to his mouth, it's all the invitation I need. I reach across his office desk and place both hands on his button-down, lifting him from his office chair.

"What the hell did you do, Dad?"

"Shepherd, let go of me," he says sternly, looking down at my hands. He glances over to the blinds of his office, assuring himself that they're closed.

When I make no move to listen, he brings his gaze back to me, then his hands encircle and forcefully shove mine away.

"Did she film this?" he asks.

"What the hell does it matter?"

"Watch your language. I'll not have you speak to me this way, boy," he says as he points a finger in my face. He then fixes his shirt and sits back down. "It *matters* because if you'd paid attention, you'd notice the clip cuts off at a rather awkward moment. The part where I pushed her off, giving her a speech about the behavior I expect from teenage girls who come under my roof, is completely, and *conveniently,* edited out. I remember the day she tried to pull that stunt but only thought she was one of your little friends. Imagine my surprise when I found she was your girlfriend."

All my anger at my father dissipates right then. I don't know if it's because he seems unbothered by the clip or because he confirmed he and Evelyn weren't together in that way. When he doesn't say anything else I ask, "Why didn't you tell me about it?"

"Because at the time, I thought it was a harmless crush. She'd tiptoe by my office and sometimes look in, saying hello every now and then. After the day I gave her the set down about her deplorable behavior—what you saw in the video— she never tried anything else, so I didn't think it was something you needed to know about. She wasn't your girlfriend at the time. If she were, I would have advised you *not* to remain with her."

"Still, Dad, you should've told me."

"I'm wondering how and why it was filmed. Did she send you that clip? " he asks, a frown creasing his brows.

"No, I don't think so. Some random number sent it to my phone, and when I showed it to her—just, no."

He looks over at me, alarmed. "What do you mean 'some random number'? You don't know who sent it to you?"

"No, I got it today."

"You confronted her about it? Did she say she sent it to someone?" he asks, a bit more alarmed now.

"Honestly, Dad, I don't know. I was so damned pissed at her that I left her house not finding out much about anything. All she told me was that the video wasn't what it looked like, which you just pretty much confirmed."

Raking his hands through his hair and bringing them down the planes of his face, he narrows his eyes. "Give me back your phone."

I hand it to him without hesitation. "What are you gonna do?"

He picks up his office phone and dials the number that sent me the video. He doesn't answer me but sits there waiting. When no one picks up, he takes a notepad and pen and jots the number down.

"Dad, you're worried, aren't you?"

"I'm getting someone to track the phone number. Since you don't know who sent it, I have a feeling they're not sending it to you for fun. Do you have *any* idea who may want to do this?"

"No. And Evelyn had no idea anyone had it, before I confronted her about it today. She was as shocked as I was."

"Obviously, whoever sent it doesn't like her ... or you for that matter."

"Why do you say that? The part about me, I mean."

"Well for starters, I'm your father. And although I know the video's harmless, doctored the way it is, it tells a completely different story," he explains. "It's incriminating."

I'd been so upset I didn't actually think about why that video was filmed. Evelyn hadn't been surprised that there *was* a video, just that it had been sent to me.

Why record it in the first place?

Chapter Twenty-One

EVIE

The moment Shepherd walks out and leaves me standing in my living room, my mind goes for a tailspin. I wipe at the onslaught of tears running down my face. Whirling around, I take the stairs two at a time to get to my bedroom. I reach for my backpack and drag out my laptop.

I search the files on it, checking if it's still there.

It is.

Intrigue, the video I'd recorded and edited, sits where I left it. I search for when the file was last opened and find that it was within the last month.

But that's impossible.

I haven't opened it since I finished the edits, which was over a month ago. I'd been saving the video for when the time came to send it in.

Who could have sent it to Shepherd?

No one knew about it, except me ... or at least I thought so.

I slide to the floor, my hands covering my face in mortification. Someone else has access to the video and I have no clue who it is.

How could they have gotten their hands on it? *Who* else could they have sent it to? *Why* did they send it to Shepherd? And how could I have been so careless?

Shepherd didn't even give me a chance to explain, to tell him that—

Tell him what, huh?

Shepherd wouldn't have given a damn. Didn't he say he didn't want to hear anything I had to say?

Fresh tears fall down my cheeks. I thought he cared about me. But the way he blazed out of here without giving me the chance to explain myself, lets me know that he'll choose his father's side, no matter what I say.

Why does it hurt this much, knowing that fact?

It doesn't matter. I *refuse* to sit here feeling sorry for myself.

Pushing up off the floor I pace my room.

Wallowing in self-pity and being emotional over this isn't going to solve anything. I need to figure this out.

I get my phone out and dial Tiffany.

"Hey, Evie, what's up?"

"Can you come over? I really need you right now?" I try to get my voice under control but fail.

"Oh my gosh, what happened?" she asks, concern evident in her voice. "I'll be right over."

I don't bother trying to explain the situation over the phone.

When Tiffany arrives less than fifteen minutes later, I'm dragging her up to my room and questioning her.

"Intrigue." I gauge her reaction to the word, needing to know she has nothing to do with this.

She looks at me expectantly. "OK. *Intrigue.* What do you mean by intrigue?" Her face is so clueless it leaves no doubt in my mind that she knows nothing about the video.

"Do you remember when I told you about Ethan?"

"Yeah, your twin brother who died. Why?"

"Do you also remember my reaction that night at the football game? When I asked you about Shepherd's dad?"

"Y—yeah ... Evie, what's this about?"

"He—he's the man who was driving drunk that night my brother was killed," I admit. "The man who walked free."

Tiffany's eyes flicker and her mouth slackens.

She walks closer to me and places her hand on my shoulder, "Are—are you sure? I mean, you were pretty young at the time."

"I'm sure, Tiffany. I'd recognize his face anywhere."

"How come you're just mentioning this now?" she asks, still not quite convinced.

"Because"—turning away from her, I go over to stand by my laptop—"I did something. But someone got their hands on it. And God knows what they're planning on doing with it."

"Evie, you're freaking me out. What exactly did you do?"

"Promise you won't judge me. I mean, you said it your-self that the bastard who killed my brother needed to pay, right?"

When she says nothing, I let it all out. I tell her every-thing, from the plan, to how I used Shepherd to get to his dad. I explain how Shepherd found out through the video someone sent him. How he blew up and pretty much hates me now.

"And now someone has the video and I have no idea who it could be," I finish.

"Evie, this is … a lot." Tiffany sits on the edge of my bed. She picks up my laptop and plays the video. Once it finishes she looks up at me. "What happened after that? You didn't go all the way with his dad did you?"

"Of course not! I wouldn't have done that. Plus, Mr. Buchanan stopped me. When you saw him put his hands on me, it was to push me off him."

"Do your parents know about this?"

"God no! They don't even know Shepherd's dad. My dad only ever met his stepmom."

"So wait. You never told your parents that the guy you're *dating* is the son of the man who killed your brother?" she asks, her eyebrows raised in surprise.

"Tiffany, they don't even know I'm dating—was dating Shepherd. I don't think we're still together. Not after this." I walk over to her, pluck my laptop from her hands and close it. "Look, right now my only concern is finding out who has the damned video. Although, I don't know how much of that should concern me at this point. I'm still bringing it in."

"What! Evie, you can't be serious," she says, flying off the bed and over to me.

"If I don't, this will all have been for nothing. Ethan's murderer will stay a free man, and I can't do that to his memory. That sick bastard has to pay," I say to her, almost pleading. "I don't care what Shepherd thinks of me anymore."

She hugs me to her. "I won't say that I agree with your methods, because I don't. I can't imagine anyone causing my brother's death and getting away with it. I would want revenge as much as you do. I just hope you don't end up hurting yourself in the process."

"I don't feel anything for Shepherd so that's impossible," I say, not sure if I'm trying to convince her or myself.

"Have you thought about what you're gonna tell your parents once they find out about all this? The video, I mean, when you take it into the cops?"

"No." I wanted to shield my parents from the truth as much as possible. I hadn't thought about how I would prevent them from finding out about all this when I eventually did bring the video in.

I guess I'll have to cross that bridge when I get there.

When I get home from school the next day, the first thing I notice is a white Benz in my driveway.

Shepherd's here.

What the hell?

He wasn't at school, so I didn't expect him to come today. Not after how he reacted to the video that was sent to him. Not after he said those horrible things to me.

As soon as Dad parks, I'm out of the truck and opening the front door.

"What's the rush?" Dad asks, stepping down from the truck.

"We don't know how long Shepherd's been waiting. You always tell me that being a good host is priority when guests are over."

"OK," he says, suspicion lacing his voice.

Entering the house, I resume my mission to find out why the hell Shepherd still decided to show up here for tutoring after the fallout we'd had less than twenty-four hours ago.

I search the living room, dining room, and the den.

When I find no sign of him, I go out back to where my mom does her gardening.

Maybe that's where he went.

Once outside, I find my mom pulling weeds from around one of her pansies, but there's no one else with her. "Mom, where is Shepherd?"

"I'm not sure. I left him in the living room. Is he not there?"

"No." As soon as I reply, a thought comes to me, and as rapidly as it comes, I take off just as fast. I run back into the house, then fly up the stairs and make a beeline for my bedroom.

When I open my door, I see Shepherd bent over one of my journals.

"What are you doing here?" I ask, breathless as I approach him.

He brings his attention to me, an expression akin to confusion mixed with ... awe on his face. It's unmistakable that he's been reading through the pages.

"Who's Ethan?" The question is innocent, and it almost distances him from the events of that awful day.

Almost.

Irritated, I grab my journal from him. "This is *private*." I bring the journal to my chest. "Get out." I walk over to my bedroom window in an attempt to create some space between us.

He makes no move to leave. "You're the last person to suggest that something remain private. What you tried to do with my dad was *disgusting* and you should be ashamed of yourself. I can't even believe I ever—"

"Are you here to tell me again how much you're done with me? How much you have no interest in seeing or talking to me? Because if that's the case, why the hell are you even here? In *my* house, in *my* room," I demand, inter-rupting him.

"You think I wanna be here, Evelyn? I'm only here to get answers, since you weren't so forthcoming with them the first time. I asked you a question. Who's Ethan?" He glares at me.

I want to tell him I don't care to give him any answers, but since he's going to find out anyway, I tell him. "He's my brother."

"Your brother?" He frowns in confusion. "Where is he? And how come you've never talked about him? How come we've never seen him?"

"*Was* my brother. He's dead."

He's silent for a moment. "Um, I'm sorry," he states, clearing his throat. "How did he die?"

"Look, you didn't come here for us to have polite conversation, so can we cut to the chase already?" I don't want to talk about Ethan. Not with him, and certainly not right now.

"Why'd you film the video?" he asks, his voice cold. He probably wants to be over with this just as much as I do.

"Easy. Why do we do half the things we do? Because I *wanted* to." I avert my gaze and walk over to the nightstand closest to the window. I place my journal inside the top drawer, closing it.

"Bullshit. You expect me to believe you have a kink for my dad. So you filmed yourself making out with him, for what, keeps?"

"You can believe whatever you want, Shepherd." I'm over this conversation, and no matter what he says or tries to convince me of, I'm still going ahead with my plan. *Nothing* he says or does at this point will prevent me from doing what I'd set out to do. I may have failed with him, but his dad was a success. I'm taking the video in to the police station as soon as Tiffany gets here. "Your *dad* was into it just as much as I was," I continue in a detached voice. My back to him, I peer through the open slits of my blinds, looking for any trace of Tiffany's car coming up our street.

I don't hear him come up behind me. Shepherd jerks me around to face him. My palms fly up, pushing at him to let me go.

He captures my wrists. "If you honestly think my dad has a thing for you, you're *delusional*," he grinds out, his face flushed and inches from mine.

"That's not what it felt like when his lips were pressed —" I don't get to finish.

Shepherd thrusts me away from him so hard I stumble, falling back against the blinds. "From now on you're more than welcome to give yourself to whomever you choose," he says in a voice void of emotion. "Don't ever call me. Don't ever text me. *Lose* my number." He strides to my bedroom door and is about to leave but utters words that send me into a spiral. "Oh and by the way, you should know that the little ploy of yours to seduce my dad was completely useless. He has surveillance installed in his office. So that stunt you pulled to make it seem like he has a *thing* for you will get you nowhere."

When he walks out, I'm frozen, my mind reeling.

That can't be true.

When the front door slams downstairs, I drop to the floor, staring into nothingness.

It can't be true.

I'd scoped out Mr. Buchanan's office but never thought to look if he had hidden cameras of his own in there. Of course he would, someone that foul, that calculating ...

When reality hits me, I feel ill.

Everything.

Everything I've done has all been for nothing.

For the next couple of school days, Shepherd tries to make my life hell.

For someone who says he wants nothing to do with me, he sure as hell has a strange way of showing it.

Once, he corners me in one of the stairwells before third period.

"If you think I care about you flirting with Elliot in front of me, I couldn't give less of a shit." Shepherd grabs hold of my arm.

"I wasn't flirting with Elliot," I try explaining to him, but stop myself because I don't have to anymore.

"Whatever, *E-vie*. Like I said, I don't give a damn." He releases my arm, then continues up the stairs.

Shepherd comes after me again during lunch. I'm walking with Tiffany and Casey when he knocks my shoulder, causing me to drop my lunch tray.

He's back to treating me the way he had when I started attending school here.

Only this time, it's worse.

It's affecting me more. The way he looks at me with such hatred. Eyes that once watched me with interest, trust, love.

I hate it.

"Didn't you say it was a game?" Tiffany asks as we head to our lockers.

I said that, but I only wish ... "Yeah, it was a game."

"Exactly, so let it stay that way. Shepherd'll get over it. There are plenty of other guys out there."

When we get to my locker, I notice there's a poster

stuck to it. I realize the same poster is randomly placed on other lockers lining the hallway. I stare at it and my mouth falls open, all the blood draining from my face.

The poster shows a still image from the video that was sent to Shepherd's phone. My face is blurred, but you can still tell it's me, while Mr. Buchanan's head is completely hidden. There's a tagline in red that reads, "AND THE SLUT OF THE YEAR AWARD GOES TO ..."

"What the—?" Tiffany immediately snatches the poster from her locker. "They're everywhere, Evie!"

My ears start ringing and I can't take my eyes off the poster.

I don't care who you're with. Don't ever call me. Don't ever text me. Lose my number.

Shepherd.

He did this. I know it had to be him who posted all these. I was dead to him. Why would he care if he ruined my life? I tried to ruin his dad's life, and now he's returning the favor.

Everyone's eyes are on me, but I manage to keep my composure.

Holding myself together, I turn away from the lockers, not bothering to collect my books.

I try to go throughout my day like nothing's happened. During lunch, people whisper about me, looking at me with hateful stares. I don't see Shepherd. As a matter of fact, I haven't seen him all day.

Coward.

If he's going to do all this, then he should at least have the decency to show up. Revel in his victory over me.

Crush me.

I get called to the principal's office before fifth period, and once I arrive, my parents are already there.

"I don't understand how such an image of your daughter could have been taken had she not been a willing participant, Mr. Richards," Mr. Bailey, our school principal, says. "Based on the image and the recording, it is very clear that she isn't without fault in this."

"Evelyn!" My mom notices me at the door.

I'm so embarrassed all I want to do is shrink to the size of an atom and disappear.

I take a seat between my parents at Mr. Bailey's direction.

"Mr. Buchanan should be here in the next five minutes."

What?

Mortified, I sit there, Dad glaring at me, his disappointment visible beneath his anger.

When Mr. Buchanan walks in, my parents go rigid.

Yeah.

Now they know Shepherd Buchanan is the sole son of Mr. Michael Buchanan, the man who caused their son's death.

So here we are.

Mr. Buchanan recognizes my parents. But instead of showing discomfort, he turns his head this way and that, and realization dawns on him. I can see when the theory crystallizes in his head, giving him the motive behind my actions.

"Now, all parties are here," Mr. Bailey says. "I will show the recording, as well as footage from Mr. Buchanan's office cameras."

After about five minutes of tape, viewing the incident from various angles, they all determine that I plotted and schemed to get Mr. Buchanan in a compromising position. My parents are disappointed as hell.

"I don't want to go back to school," I say when we're in the car on our way home.

The principal suspended me for a week, but I have zero motivation to stay in a place where everyone looks at me the way they did today.

"Evie, you made decisions without us and we will make some without you," my dad says firmly. "Did you know Shepherd was that man's son?"

"I've known for a while."

"Why didn't you tell us?" Mom asks, sadness coating her voice.

"Because I didn't want you both revisiting all the pain I did when *I* found out." I look at my dad through the rearview mirror. "Dad, please, I don't want to go back. Someone posted pictures of us all over people's lockers at school."

"I know," he says ruefully.

"So then why—?"

"We won't be sending you back to school next week, but we've discussed hiring a therapist."

"*What?*"

"Evie, you need one. Ethan's death was a traumatic experience that I don't think any of us have fully healed from. And what you've done is indicative of deeper-seated issues that neither your mom nor I can help you with."

"Dad. Come on, look at me. I don't need a therapist."

"It's not what we look like," he states, then points to his head. "It's about what's going on up here. We need a level of peace up here to function in a healthy way in this world. It's vital for developing healthy friendships, relationships, and trust."

I snort. "I don't see myself trusting anyone anytime

soon. Least of all some stranger coming to psychoanalyze me."

"Evie," my mom warns.

"What? No, Mom, I'm serious. I'm not seeing a *therapist*." I put the word in air quotes, rolling my eyes.

"Well then it's back to school," my dad says flatly.

I weigh my options.

Although I hate the notion of seeing a shrink, I hate the idea of stepping another foot back into that school even more.

"Alright fine, whatever. I'll see a therapist. But only for like a week."

"No. For as long as it takes." My dad refocuses on the road.

"Well, what if that's like, I don't know, for the rest of my life?"

"Well then I guess a lifetime is what it'll take."

I groan, staring out my window.

Outside, the trees' leaves change in color from vivid green to the dull browns of fall.

Chapter Twenty-Two

SHEPHERD

Evelyn doesn't show up to school.

Good.

The last thing I need is her presence here reminding me of everything, especially that video. I need bleach to get rid of those images.

The whole school knows about it too. Though people haven't seen the video, they've seen the posters. It didn't take Sherlock Holmes to figure out it was her in the photo.

I don't know who posted them, but it's probably the same person who sent me the video.

As if all that isn't enough, everyone looks at me with these pitying stares for having a girlfriend cheat on me with an older guy.

A week goes by and Evelyn still doesn't show up. I should be happy about it, but it doesn't sit well with me.

"You doing OK, man?" Lucas asks as he sits at our table after getting his lunch.

"Every day's a new day." I push at the spaghetti, then grab the apple off my tray.

Beanca gets to our table, but Jones isn't with her.

"Hey, where's Jones?" I ask

She looks at me with that *you know* expression.

I roll my eyes, tossing my apple back onto the tray. I stand up to leave.

"Shep, please," Beanca says as she grabs hold of my forearm.

"Jones needs to learn who's priority," Lucas says, looking over at Beanca. "He went to see her probably."

"Look I don't give a shit who he spends his time with," I say. I open my palm to Beanca and she places her hand in mine. "What do you say we go see a movie tonight?"

She nods without hesitation.

I know. I'm a jerk. Beanca has held a candle for me for a while. I'm taking her up on it. She's available and I'm available. There's no reason two perfectly single people shouldn't have some fun together.

Lucas looks at her, then at me and says, "As long as you guys know what you're doing."

"Whatever, Lucas," she replies.

We both leave the cafeteria.

We hit the movies a few hours later, and I immediately regret it.

Beanca's trying too hard. We get popcorn and she tries to feed it to me.

I stop her.

While we're watching the movie, she places her hand on my thigh.

I brush it off.

She tries to tell me something but places her lips too close to my ear.

I lean my head away.

"What's wrong?" she asks, frustrated.

"Nothing." I gesture to the screen. "Let's just focus on the movie."

"Shep, I want to cheer you up." She smooths her hand down my arm where it lies on the armrest, then places her hand over mine. "I don't want to see you moping around like this all the time."

"Who the hell's moping around?"

A few people glance over at us, annoyed that we're talking during the movie.

"You," she whispers, bringing her face closer to mine. "We've all noticed it, so don't look all shocked."

"Bullshit."

"Could you guys keep it down?" A guy seated a row below us turns his irritated gaze our way in the darkened theatre room. "Some of us actually want to watch the movie."

I'm about to give him the finger, when Beanca clamps her other hand over my fingers. "Shep, no."

I don't know if it's feeling restrained that pisses me off or the fact that she suggested people have noticed me moping that does it, but the next thing I know I'm standing up and walking out.

"Shep, where are you going?" She tries to whisper but ends up being louder than others can manage I guess because a few more people yell for us to be quiet.

I'm halfway to the door when she grabs on to my arm, trying to keep up with my strides.

Once we're out of the theater, she whirls me around to face her. "What the hell is your problem?" she asks, exasperated. "I'm so tired of walking on eggshells around you. I mean, it's *exhausting*."

"What the hell are you talking about, Bee?" At this point I'm confused. First she tells me I've been sulking and now she tells me she's on eggshells.

"Ever since you broke up with Evie it's like you're so damned bitchy all the time."

"Oh get off it." I turn, walking away from her. I don't need this shit, not from her, not from anyone. And the last person I want to think about right now is Evelyn.

"No, to hell with you and that pole you've got stuck up your ass. I'm tired of trying to be careful around you. Evie played you. She *played* you. She didn't care about you at all. And that's why you're pissed."

I'm in front of her so fast she jumps, her eyes widening.

"Don't talk about shit you have no idea about." I glare at her. "You don't know shit about my relationship with Evelyn."

"Oh yeah," she counters, a smug look lining her features. "Well I know she had a thing for your dad. If those posters had anything to say about it, she probably messed with both him and you at the same time."

"Beanca, shut the *hell* up!" I shout. "She didn't sleep with my dad."

"How do you know that, huh? Did your little *slutty* ex-girlfriend tell you that?" There's no love lost between Beanca and Evelyn, but the animosity in Beanca's eyes gives me pause.

Frowning, I attempt to drop the conversation. But when I start walking away, Beanca sidles up next to me and tries to apologize. "I'm sorry. I just hate seeing you like this, that's all. I want the old Shep back. The one who'd smile and flirt and be … normal. I hate that she did this to you. I wish she'd just, disappear."

"She already did that, Bee," I reply as we head to my car.

"No, I mean it. She's in your head so she's not gone," she counters. "I *wish* that girl would go back to wherever the hell she came from, that she never came to our school."

A sharp sensation stabs at my chest at her words.

I'm grateful for Beanca's loyalty to me, but the thought of never having met Evelyn, never seeing her again, makes me feel off.

When another two weeks go by and Evelyn still doesn't show up to school, I try to force myself not to care. I keep telling myself that I don't care what happens to her as long as she stays gone.

But when two weeks turn into three, I decide to ask the school counselor about her, just out of curiosity. Of course, she can't tell me much, only that Evelyn wouldn't be returning until after winter break.

I should feel good about that.

But I don't.

Should be grateful at the news.

But I'm not.

Why did hearing that she'd left school for the rest of the semester irritate the shit out of me? I'd wanted her out of my sight, but it wasn't like her to ditch school for so long.

I need to find out what's up with her. I whip out my phone to check social media and realize that in my anger I'd deleted her from every single one of my accounts.

Damn it.

And of course all hers are private.

School gets out a few hours later, and I check the bookstore she hangs out at sometimes.

Nothing.

I go to the park she spends time at when she writes.

Not there either.

I decide to drive by her house. Yup, definitely not a stalker at all.

As soon as I get there, I notice Jones's Porsche in her driveway.

Great.

I should drive away. She's obviously OK. From the looks of it, she's not in any kind of trouble if she has Jones still visiting her all the damned time.

Before I think better of it, I kill the engine. I sit there, my hands clenching and unclenching the steering wheel.

Sometime later, I sit up when her front door opens. Jones appears and looks behind him. He notices no one's there and goes back inside. Seconds pass and he reemerges, holding on to Evelyn's hands and pulling her away from the front door.

Finally seeing her after so long does crazy things to my chest. My thoughts are all jumbled as I watch them at the front of her house. I don't like how intimate they seem with each other. I don't know if I'm upset, or what, but my heart starts pounding in my ears.

I try to get a good look at Evelyn, but I can't see her face from where I'm parked on the opposite side of the street.

Jones tries to get her to his car, and I'm opening my door. It's like my legs take on a mind of their own and carry me over to them.

"What's up!" I shout, approaching them, like I have every right to be there.

Evelyn turns to look at me. Her eyes flinch and her body stiffens. Instead of the sadness I saw there just a few seconds ago, she masks her features, her expression blank. It's like she's looking through and not at me.

Jones, who's surprised to find me standing there, narrows his eyes.

"I saw your car and remembered I needed to ask you about something," I lie, looking between him and Evelyn.

"This isn't a good time, Shep," he says. "Let's talk later."

At this point, I haven't said anything to Evelyn. I could turn and walk away, but something keeps my feet rooted to the ground. I turn to her and ask, "How are you doing? I haven't seen you around school lately."

"Shepherd, I told you to leave," Jones insists, his voice laced with irritation and some other emotion, as if he's attempting to shield her from me.

Ignoring him, I continue watching Evelyn, waiting for her to respond. I need her to say something to me. It's been a month since I've seen her, heard her voice, and maybe I just need her to acknowledge that I'm here.

She still doesn't answer me. She averts her gaze, but not before I witness the sadness returning to her brown eyes.

"Are you OK?" After all she's done to my dad, to me, the last thing I should care about is how she's doing.

"Jones." Her voice is quiet. "I'm sorry, I can't—I just, I can't—" She immediately turns away, racing back into the house.

"Evie, no." Jones reaches for her but catches air. "Get out of here," he directs at me before turning to go back in after her.

Oh hell no.

I grab hold of his shoulder. "What the hell is wrong with Evelyn?"

"Bro, are you really gonna stand there and ask me that?"

"What? What are you talking about, Jones?" I'm confused by his question.

"If you don't know what's 'wrong' with Evie, let me spell it out for you. Y-O-U. *You're* what's wrong with her," he says, shoving me in the chest.

"What does that mean?"

"If you wanna know, you can go ask her," he says. When he sees my reaction to his words, he shakes his head and looks away.

I'm pretty sure Evelyn doesn't want to see me, if the way she just ran away from me is any indication.

"Between the two of us, she's still beating herself up over everything that happened," Jones continues. "It's affecting her a lot more than she'll admit. More than anything though, she needs to know she has friends who still care about her. And Shep"—he looks back at me—"for what it's worth, she misses you, man."

I freeze.

I *didn't* expect him to say that. I don't know how to feel. "Did *she* tell you that?"

"Not in so many words. But it's in what she doesn't say," he replies.

"Yeah, well, the shit she pulled with my dad was pretty messed up."

"Have you asked her *why* she did all that?"

"She told me she wanted to do it. What more is there to ask? Evelyn admitted she used me. She said those words to me, verbatim."

"Shep—"

"Later, Jones." I walk away without giving him the

chance to finish. I don't want anyone trying to convince me of Evelyn's supposed guilt over what happened. I can't forget the crazy shit she did.

I won't.

She really misses you, man.

I contemplated going to her in that moment. Hell, it's hard preventing myself from doing that right now. Raking my hands through my hair, I slam a fist against the hood of my car.

"Damn it!"

Jerking my door open, I slide behind the wheel, then glance over at Evelyn's house. I start up the car, pull out, then tear down the street, leaving Jones there. Let him take care of her.

I'd told *E-vie* I was through with her, and I'd meant it.

EVIE

I watch Shepherd speed away.

Seeing him again brought back so many memories. The good times, before ...

I *feel* so much. But to my surprise, my eyes are dry. Maybe I'm empty of tears.

I want to scream.

I want to break something.

Nothing worked out the way it was supposed to. Fate played me like a fiddle. She's laughing at me. Laughing that she's pulled one over on me again.

"*God*, help me," I whisper into the emptiness of my room. "I failed us both, didn't I, Ethan?"

Jones comes back into the house and finds me in my room. I try to smile and tell him I'm OK. Of course he sees right through it.

He also notices that I don't want to talk. He settles on the beanbag in my bedroom.

I don't have the heart to keep him around, especially when I know I'm only going to be negative. "Jones, I want to be alone."

"I don't think that's a good idea."

"Look, my mom and dad are going to be here any minute, so you can leave. I won't do anything crazy." I wouldn't do anything to hurt myself, but Jones doesn't trust that. I don't know what gave him the impression that I would do anything to harm myself.

He's been hanging around me a lot lately, ever since I stopped going to school.

I do my classwork online and submit it to my teachers that way. The school granted me the ability to finish the semester this way because of all that happened. The guidance counselor suggested that I see a professional, so my dad let them know he'd hired me a therapist.

I've been going to talk therapy and it's helped in its own way, but I still feel guilty about my brother. I'm having a hard time coping with everything, and seeing Shepherd today ... makes it feel like I've been knocked back a few paces.

I didn't know I could care this much about a guy, especially since I've believed myself incapable of it. I hate how Shepherd makes me feel guilty as hell when he's around. I wanted to go to him, wrap my arms around him and tell him how sorry I am. That it's because of what his dad did that I thought I needed to get revenge.

I told my therapist I wanted Shepherd to hurt for laughing at us when I was eight and his father got off. She explained that his reaction was normal for a son who was happy his father was going home. She said at that age, he wouldn't have known to grieve for someone else's family, especially for a boy he never knew.

I place a fist against my chest, because thoughts of Ethan assail my brain. When I start thinking about how Mr. Buchanan still hasn't paid for what he did, it makes me ill.

"Damn it!" I yell.

"What is it, Evie?" Jones comes to me and takes a hold of my hands, removing them from my face. "What's wrong?"

I'm angry and disillusioned with everything. I set out to bring justice to my brother, and all I ended up doing was hurting myself and the one other person I came to care for in the process.

Shepherd didn't deserve any of this.

He deserves love, honesty.

But we were doomed the two us, doomed in love. He deserves so much better than me.

Ethan deserves better than me.

I drag my hands from his and start beating at my chest, hoping the physical pain will lessen the hurt.

"Evie, stop it. Please stop," Jones says as he grabs hold of my fist. When he hugs me, I fall into him, a shudder racking my body. "Cry it out. Don't leave any of it inside."

I let it all out then, and it's like a dam breaks.

When the tears finally subside, I look up at him through puffy eyes.

"I'm gonna call Tiffany. You'll need her more than me tonight." After he calls her, he gets me some tissues to clean up.

"Evie," he says, pausing before he continues, "Shepherd doesn't hate you."

"He should," I reply. "I don't know if anyone would still

care about me, if I did to them what I've done to him." I wipe at my nose.

"I've seen him. I know him, and he's in love with you."

"Jones, stop. I know you're trying to help, but don't."

He doesn't say anything else and I'm relieved.

It'll be just like old times, when Shepherd and I had nothing.

End of.

Chapter Twenty-Three

SHEPHERD

"Are you familiar with a Beanca Carlyle?" The guy my dad hired to trace the burner phone that sent the video is finally getting back to me.

I'm in the middle of packing for a ski trip to Colorado. I won't be back until after the new year. "Hey, yeah I am. Why?" I ask, the phone at my ear. I fold clothes and pack away some of my gear. I'm about to stuff more jackets into my suitcase, when the guy's next words chill me.

"Ms. Carlyle is the one who purchased the phone in question."

I pause mid-fold, forgetting the jackets in my hand. "I'm sorry, what?" I ask, puzzled. "That's impossible."

"My records show that on the eleventh of November, the phone was purchased at a local store, not too far from your school. The purchaser used a credit card under the name of a Rebecca Carlyle. *The* Mrs. Carlyle was at home at the time of the sale, as was her husband and youngest daughter. That leaves the eldest child, Beanca Carlyle. The

CCTV footage of the local cell phone retailer shows that at around 5:53 p.m., Ms. Carlyle made the purchase. That phone was the same one used to send you the video not too long after."

I'm silent as I try to wrap my mind around what he's saying.

"If you have any questions please don't hesitate to ask. I trust you know that I'm very thorough," he says.

"Is there any way you could send me footage of her buying the phone?"

"Not a problem at all. You'll have it within the next few minutes."

"Thanks," I say stiffly. I drop my jackets on the bed and pace the length of my bedroom.

Why would Beanca of all people have a copy of the video? How the hell did she get it?

When I hear the notification, I immediately check the message.

I hit play and as soon as the video starts I see Beanca's signature ponytail and PSA uniform as she enters the store. One angle reveals that it's so unmistakably her, I find myself staggering over to sit on my bed. I watch as she talks to the store clerk, then he displays three phones. She picks one and then makes the purchase.

I put the phone down, sitting on the side of my bed for what feels like an eternity, trying to understand Beanca's motive. The video, the posters around the school. And then my head latches on to an idea.

She's had growing feelings for me and I knew that, but I would never think Beanca capable of something like this. It was low.

I pick up my phone and dial her number.

She picks up on the third ring. "Hey, Shep. What's up?"

"Can you come over to my place?"

"Why? What's up?"

"I've got something I have to run by you. It won't take long."

"OK sure. I'll be there in twenty."

I'm calm as I wait for her to get here.

When she arrives, I'm downstairs so fast my feet barely touch the stairs.

I let her in.

She's smiling at me until I shove my phone in her face and hit play.

"You want you to explain to me what you were doing at that store?" I ask, daring her to lie to me as I stare into her vivid green eyes.

"I was buying a phone, duh." She avoids eye contact and twists her fingers into her ponytail.

"Yeah? What happened to the phone?"

"I threw it out. Decided to keep my old one since it was obvious trash."

"Hmm." I move closer to her and lean down to whisper in her ear. "Did you know someone found it?"

When I move my head so I can look at her face, her eyes widen.

"Did you also know that that person got a hold of a nasty little video? And out of all the people in the world they could send it to, they happened to have my number available?" I ask sarcastically, circling her. "Now I'm curious. If that phone was such *obvious trash*, why did it have a video in pristine condition of my dad and my ex-girlfriend on it? A video, by the way, that was filmed at least a month before the purchase of said phone."

"I—I don't know. Maybe someone fished it out of the trash when I tossed it in and they—"

"I'm not an *idiot*, Beanca!" I bark at her. "Now," I continue calmly, my hands steepled at my mouth. "Why don't you tell me what happened? How did you get the video, huh? Oh and Bee, don't leave any of it out. We have all evening." I relax my stance, folding my arms out in front of me and leaning against the entryway table.

She sputters into speech. "It was Evie. She was the one who recorded that repulsive video. I only—"

"Beanca," I warn. "Please, don't try to tell me things I already know. Let's start at the beginning. Better yet, let's start with what happened *before* you decided that we all needed to know about it."

She starts the story further back than I thought she'd go, and some of the things she reveals catch me off guard. "I saw that you had real feelings for her," she says. "And you were different than you'd been with the others, Chase, Lexie—just *different*. At least with them I knew you weren't invested in any real relationship.

But you started changing, started softening toward Evie, and you two were barely even friends. It was one thing when you'd ignore her, but then you started being mean to her and you're not like that with girls. You're either indifferent or you're interested." When I'm about to interrupt her, she puts a hand up to stop me.

"Let me finish. Do you remember that night at the homecoming afterparty?" I nod once. "You stayed out there with her after you and Jones got into that huge fight, because of *her*. That's when I realized you had feelings for her. Otherwise you wouldn't have done all that, gotten into a fight with a friend over a girl you weren't interested in. Only, you weren't aware you had feelings for her then."

"So you decided you didn't like her because of that?

Something she had no control over? Evelyn couldn't control whether I was interested in her or not," I argue.

"Exactly. And that's why when she went from hating you to tutoring you, wanting to be your friend suddenly, I got suspicious. I know girls, Shep. We don't do that unless we're after something. I would watch how she was with you in group settings, and even though you didn't see it, there was something singular about the way she was with you, almost calculating. At least, at first."

"What do you mean?"

She brushes a hand over her hair in frustration. "Obviously she started liking you. That's what pushed me over the edge. She was taking away any chance of us being together." When she says this I want to tell her that even without Evelyn around, I still wouldn't see her as anything more than a friend. But now is not the time.

"Anyway, I followed her to study hall one day, a day that her friend Tiffany wasn't there. When she stepped out to use the restroom or something, I snooped on her computer. I'd been suspicious of her and, I don't know, something told me to go over and check it out. No one paid any attention to me, so I sat there looking through her stuff. Then I saw this video file with the name *Intrigue*. I had no idea what it was, so I clicked on it out of curiosity. That's when I saw the video of her and your dad. I didn't hesitate after that. I sent myself the video through her email account and then erased all record of having sent it."

I look at Beanca through new eyes, the rose-colored glasses now taken off. "And you didn't think *that* would have been the appropriate time to tell me? As soon as you found the video?"

"I wanted to, Shep. Believe me, I did."

"Sure."

She holds on to my arm. "I'm not lying. I *did*. But I thought about all you'd been through with your family. I didn't want you looking at your dad any worse than you already had."

"Oh bullshit, Beanca. Give me a break. You don't give a damn about my dad or our relationship," I counter.

"I *do*," she pleads.

"So then why'd you reveal the video the way you did, huh? Why didn't you come tell me, instead of sending it to me through a burner phone, like some lurker creeping in the shadows?"

"Because—"

I don't give her the chance to come up with some lame excuse. "I'll tell you. Because you didn't want to run the risk of me asking how long you'd been sitting on that video. The only reason you sent that shit to me was because you saw me getting close to Evelyn and you didn't like it. Admit it."

When she remains silent, I have my answer.

"But you didn't stop there, did you? It wasn't enough that we'd broken up. You tried to destroy Evelyn by printing those disgusting images for the whole damned school to see. You knew she'd assume it was me. Man, when you decide to kill something you don't just twist the knife do you? You slice it up too."

"Shep," she says brokenly, the telltale sign of tears forming in her eyes. "I'm sorry."

"No the hell you're not," I interrupt. "Someone who's sorry doesn't do all that planning and scheming only to apologize when they're caught."

Out of her and Evelyn, I don't know who's worse.

"Shep, please," she pleads.

"Just get out. I need time to think things through." I'm

too affected right now and there's only one tiny ass string left before I completely snap.

She doesn't move so I nudge her all the way to and through my front door. I slam it behind her, lock it and climb the stairs two at a time to get to my room.

I'm through with this fake bullshit. People showing me one side of their personality, while doing something different under the table. I can't do it anymore. Where are the chicks who when I'm with them, what I see is what I get?

I reach for my phone and call Lexie. When I was with her, there was no doubt what we were to one another. No strings, just fun.

I could use some of that.

Chapter Twenty-Four

EVIE

Chase is throwing another house party. Of course I have no interest in going, because chances are, *he* will be there. But when I find out from Jones that Shepherd's heading out of town early, I accept Jones's offer to come with.

I haven't been going out a lot because I'm still healing from what happened. Things haven't blown over yet, at least not for me. And even though I haven't been to school, I've still been picky about which groups I'm around. After winter break's over, I can return to PSA without worrying about randoms talking about me or giving me nasty looks.

At least the people Chase hangs around aren't judgy, so I don't have much to worry about tonight.

It's chilly now that the season's changed, so I throw on a leather jacket and scarf, before heading out. Tiffany and Casey are in the car when Jones gets me. They're official now, finally having pushed past the friendship stage.

We step inside Chase's place, and it's not as crowded as

it usually is this time of night. I don't know how to feel about that because larger crowds are easier to disappear into. Smaller, intimate ones make you stick out like a sore thumb.

"Hey, Tiff!" Some girl comes over and hugs Tiffany. I've seen her before, but I can't pinpoint where. Tiffany introduces us and the two of them start sharing secrets.

I'm the third wheel, so I turn to Jones. We walk to one of the corners of the living room and sit and talk about what he's doing for winter break. I'm staying in town, while he'll only be here for half the time. He's visiting family up in Baltimore but will be back in time for New Year's.

At least I'll have one friend in town for part of the holidays. I don't know yet what Tiffany is doing, but as I look over at where she's standing with Casey, I don't expect her to have much time to hang out with me.

Jones places a hand over mine. "Hey, heads-up. Shep said he wasn't gonna be here, honest to God." I don't realize Shepherd has entered the house until he whispers this to me.

I instantly look over to the front door, and sure enough Shepherd's there, talking to one of his teammates. He doesn't notice me, but my eyes take him in. The dark blazer. His hair slicked back. He looks amazing, and my heart flutters at the sight.

I shift my gaze, deciding to pay attention instead to the fibers in the rug. The room suddenly feels warm, so I take off my jacket and place it over the chair. I spot Elliot waving at me and smile in greeting.

He's with a group of friends from the lacrosse team. He says something to them before heading over. "Hey, Evie. It's been a while. You're good?" He reaches down to hug me, and I get up so it's not awkward.

His inquiry is genuine, and I allow him as honest an answer as I can muster. "I'm hanging in there. Hoping to get back after break."

"I've missed you," he admits. "Have you gone to any more poetry slams?"

"Not yet."

"Bummer. Your stuff is legit." His compliment brightens my mood.

"Thanks, Elliot. That means a lot," I reply with a smile.

"Hey, has anyone seen Lexie?" Shepherd yells across the room

My smile falters.

Someone tells him she's in the back room so he heads in that direction, not bothering to look anywhere else.

Jones squeezes my hand.

Elliot takes the empty seat on my right and strikes up a conversation about what his family has planned for the holidays. He's loaded. His family is traveling out to Paris to visit one of his relatives. From there, they plan on traveling to Italy, then up to Germany.

"I'm jealous. I wish my parents would plan a vacation like that for us," I say.

"Same," Jones agrees. "We never go anywhere outside the four walls of the US of A. And it's not like we don't have the money. My folks said we were going to Mexico last year, but those plans fell through. They haven't planned anything since."

"Speaking of France," Elliot says, resting a hand against my knee. "You remind me of this French model I've seen in a few magazines. Sharon something."

I chuckle. "Thank you, Elliot. You look good too."

I don't hear what he says next because the music gets louder. Sia's "Cheap Thrills" blares through the speakers.

"Let's get this party *star-ted!*" Shepherd shouts, before hauling Lexie into the center of the room. A few other people scream and hoot, joining them in the middle of the room and dancing along to the music.

I try not to look at how he's holding her, how he's looking at her. I know I shouldn't care, but I do.

I get up to go anywhere else in the house where I don't have to witness the ridiculous show, but Elliot takes my hand and asks me to dance. I want to say no because I'm not interested in playing tit for tat. But if Shepherd weren't here, I wouldn't hesitate. I would dance with him.

Deciding not to change my decision because of an extra variable in the room, I accept Elliot's invitation. I allow myself to vibe to the music, averting my eyes whenever they wander over to Shepherd and Lexie.

Elliot's actually a pretty good dancer, and I like that he takes the lead as we dance together.

We're not even two full songs in before Shepherd comes out of nowhere and grabs hold of my arm.

"We need to talk," he says harshly.

"Shep—" Elliot starts.

"Don't." Shepherd interrupts his protests, glaring and pointing at him to stay where he is. He ushers me through the group of people and out of the living room. When we get to a door leading to the back patio, he opens it and pulls me through behind him.

"What are you doing here, huh?" he asks, glaring down at me. "Here I am trying to enjoy myself, before I have to pile into a jet to some family retreat in Colorado. And who do I have to run into? You."

My jaw slackens.

At first, I'm speechless.

Then something comes over me.

"Oh, I'm sorry. I didn't know I was in *your* house," I say, sarcasm dripping from every word. "Let me get this straight. You expect me to keep hiding in my house because you might end up in the same place I am? Well, I'm not doing that anymore. And for the record, I'm coming back to school next year. I don't care how much you don't want me around. You're not the center of my universe, Shepherd. You never were." I whirl around and pull at the door. But as soon as I manage to get it open, Shepherd slams his hands against it on either side of me. The door bangs against its frame, and I startle, jumping back. I land against his chest and leap forward, removing myself, before turning to face him.

"Are you trying to piss me off, Evelyn?" he asks unyielding, his gaze narrowing.

"What the hell are you talking about now?" I ask. "Explain, because I don't understand what I would get out of making you more upset at me than you already are."

The anger in his eyes dissipates, shifting to some other emotion.

I do the one thing I said I wouldn't do again.

I apologize.

"Shepherd, I'm sorry. I'm *sorry*, OK. Why can't you see that?" I plead.

"You're just like Beanca," he says, and it's as if he slapped me. "You know what she admitted to me?" he continues, "*She* was the one who got that video and sent it to me. Then she put those posters up. Only like you, she wouldn't have confessed if she hadn't gotten caught."

"Don't. Compare me. To Beanca," I grind out through gritted teeth. I shift my gaze to his chest because I hate the cynical look now present in his eyes.

"Shouldn't I?" he asks. "You both have this nasty habit of faking it with me to get whatever the hell you want."

"I didn't *fake* anything with you!" I'm emotional now, and I don't want to cry in front of him again. "I told you, I filmed that video before we were involved."

"You think I believe that? How could I believe anything you say, when you did it while you were supposedly *interested* in helping me? What a joke."

"You know what? Forget it." I school my features. "You want to punish me for what I did? Fine. You want to see the worst in me? Fine. I'm not tiptoeing around you anymore." With newfound resolve, I continue, "I'm going to take your advice. I'll go be with whoever the hell I want, and there's not a damned thing you'll be able to say or do about it. Have a nice life, Shepherd." I roughly brush his arm from the door so I can open it.

"The hell you will!"

Before I can turn the knob, I'm lifted off the ground. I fight back, struggling to get him to let me go. Within seconds, we're both soaking wet and in the backyard pool. It's so cold, my teeth start chattering. The white, thin-strapped dress I'm in does nothing to shield me from the icy water. I get to the edge of the pool and start trying to get out, but Shepherd stops me, spinning me around to face him.

"What do you want from me?" I scream. "I try to stay away from you and you make my life hell. I tell you I'm sorry and you still make my life hell. What do you wa—"

Shepherd grabs my face in his hands and covers my lips with his, moving them roughly across mine.

"You're driving me crazy," he says, his voice broken. "I'm not with you and I can't stand it. I try to get over you and it's—I can't—" He punctuates this by bringing his arms around me and squeezing me against him. Our clothes are soaked through, but the slight warmth of his kiss dispels any coldness I feel.

"You're in my head, Evelyn," he adds, a note of desperation and sadness in his voice. He starts kissing me again, slower, more gentle this time.

I return his embrace with all the longing I feel, because I want to, because *he* is what I want.

Shepherd breaks the kiss, sliding his hands to my upper arms. Shaking his head, he says, "We can't. I need time. Time to think things through." He releases me, then pushes up and over the pool's edge. Reaching down, he lifts me out of the water.

The wind hits me, and I start shivering. He takes off his blazer and squeezes as much water out of it as he can, before placing it over my shoulders.

"We need to get you out of that dress." He ushers me in front of him.

We head back into the house and I'm quiet. If it's time Shepherd needs, I'm more than willing to give it to him.

We get back to the living room, and as soon as people take one good look at us, they start asking questions.

"We fell in," I say when I realize Shepherd isn't interested in giving any explanations.

Chase offers me a change of clothes, but I refuse it. I hand Shepherd his blazer, throw on my jacket, and accept a dry towel to wrap around me. I call for a ride, and when it arrives, Shepherd walks me out.

"You didn't have to call, Evelyn. I could've taken you."

"I know, and I appreciate that," I say honestly. I want to be alone and I also want to respect what Shepherd said outside.

He needs time.

"Enjoy the time with your family. Hopefully, I'll see you around when you get back." With that, I get in the car and head home.

Chapter Twenty-Five

SHEPHERD

Spending the entire break out of town wasn't what I had in mind. But I needed to clear my head. I needed to be away from any distractions.

The whole time in Colorado, all I could think about was Evelyn. I know I shouldn't want her back in my life, but I do.

I miss her.

I miss seeing her, talking to her, hanging out with her. I miss being with her. It takes a lot for me to admit it to myself after what she did to me, to my dad.

I used you.

Those words are the hardest to get past. Even if it was when we were nothing to each other and all she was doing was helping me out, it still hurt like hell.

Why?

Why'd she do that to me? To *us*?

Those are the questions I want honest answers to. At the time I didn't want to hear anything she had to say because I was so damned angry, but I'm ready for those answers now.

When I get back from my trip, I want to head over to Evelyn's place, but Lucas shows up at my house before I'm able to.

"How was Colorado, bro? We missed you," Lucas says as I let him in.

"Sure," I say, sarcasm lacing my voice. I suspect the only thing Beanca is *missing* is the opportunity she *thought* we had of ever being together.

"Shep, she's sorry, man. Beanca knows what she did was wrong—"

"Is Jones back?" I ask, cutting him off. "I've been calling him but got nothing. He hasn't texted me back either."

Lucas looks anywhere but at me, rubbing the side of his neck.

"What?"

"He's been back since New Year's Eve," he replies, hesitant. "Spent it with her."

By *her* I'm assuming he's referring to Evelyn.

I texted her on the night of New Year's Eve. Jones must have been with her then.

My muscles stiffen, and I roll my neck to relieve the sudden tension. It's not like anything is going on between them. Jones wouldn't do that. But something about them still spending time alone together gets under my skin.

"I need to go see her," I say without preamble, flying up the stairs, leaving Lucas no choice but to rush up after me.

"You sure that's a good idea? Didn't you guys have that huge fight at Chase's party before you left?"

"Dude, I told you, that's not how it went down."

I take a quick shower and while I'm getting ready, Lucas updates me on what I've missed. Apparently, Dudley's secret girl is Chase. Which explains why he was acting all weird and standoffish with me.

"Chase never said anything about it," I say.

"No one dares to mention he's getting with her after you were with her." He says this with pursed lips. "I couldn't do it, bro. Friendships first, that's my motto. Don't get with your friends. It *always* messes things up."

"Yeah, well, for what it's worth, Dudley and I aren't *that* close. And did you tell that to Bee, because ..."

"Alright, Shep, I already told you, she feels awful about everything. Lay off her," he says, irritated.

"Whatever." I get my keys and we head downstairs.

He leaves, and I pull out from the garage and drive over to Evelyn's. I text her on my way there, and she tells me she's out but that she'll head back home to meet me.

I wait for her in the driveway.

A muscle tightens in my jaw when not twenty minutes later Jones's Porsche pulls up beside my car. I inhale, trying to calm whatever hostile emotions are flooding my chest. I get out and push my door closed a little harder than necessary. I walk around to the hood and wait for them.

When Evelyn gets out, I notice two things.

First, her hair. It's not in the long twists I've grown accustomed to but in an Afro of curls that sit on her shoulders. She's even more beautiful, and I don't mistake my reaction to seeing her after these two long weeks. It's all I can do not to walk over to her.

The second thing is the way she's dressed. She has on this skintight red dress that leaves none of the curves of her body to the imagination. She looks amazing. But it's not exactly warm out here. I look between her and Jones, and it seems like they were on a date or something.

My eyes slide to Jones when he says, "My bad, bro. I was gonna call you back, but I was with Evie."

Evelyn stares over at him in some sort of conspiratorial warning I'm not privy to. My fist clenches.

"What I *meant* is that I was showing Evie this art exhibit I wanted her to check out," he adds.

"Hey, how come you came here? Didn't you just get back?" Evelyn approaches me and brings her arms around my waist.

I hug her back, inhaling the scent of her hair, her skin … her.

"Am I not allowed to come here now?" I ask, a little harsher than I meant.

Evelyn instantly releases me. A look of confusion crosses her features.

"Shep," Jones starts, warning me.

I didn't come here for a fight, so I school myself into a state of calm before I respond.

"I hope *you* guys rang in the New Year well. Heard you were together then, too," I state. I'm trying here, but I'm not going to act like I'm not annoyed at what I'm seeing.

"Shepherd, what're you saying?" Evelyn asks, brows knitting together. "What are you trying to imply right now?"

"Are you guys together? Is that why you're dressed like that? You were on some kind of date? Did I interrupt or …?"

"Are you serious? Don't be a jerk?" Jones says, getting close enough to shove at me.

When I move to push at him, Evelyn stops me. "Stop!" she commands, and we both turn to look at her. "Shepherd, I told you to take as much time as you needed. But if that's not—if that's not going to work, if you're going to believe the worst about me whenever you're given the chance, then we don't have anything to say to each other." She turns to Jones, then adds, "I'm sorry."

"Evelyn," I say, grasping hold of her arm as she starts toward the house. "We need to talk."

"If you're going to be like *this*," she responds, gesturing at me with her free hand, "then we don't have anything to talk about. Let me go." She tries to pull free from me.

"Alright. I'm sorry."

"'Bout time," Jones states. "Listen, I'll let you two work this one out. Evie, call me." He puts his hand to his ear and turns to go back to his car but pauses. "Oh and, Shep, I'll call you later."

I turn to Evelyn, whose hand I still haven't let go of, and walk us to her front door.

She opens up and I head in behind her. "How was your trip?" she asks, putting her key on the hook. She holds on to the wall as she unstraps her heels.

Her back to me, I watch her.

"It was OK, I guess. Got to see family I haven't seen since last year so that was pretty cool." I notice her parents aren't home because I haven't heard anything since we got in, save for the sound of the heater. "Your folks aren't in?"

"No, after New Year's they went down to Marietta for the weekend. I wasn't feeling the trip so I stayed back." She doesn't look at me but walks barefoot on the cold tiles toward the stairs.

I don't think—I kick off my shoes, then scoop her up in my arms and carry her the rest of the way to the stairs.

"Shepherd, what are you doing?" She brings her arms around my neck for balance. "I can walk. Put me down."

"I know that. But the floor's cold, and you've got no shoes on."

"The stairs are carpeted," she says once we're on the steps.

"I may as well bring you the rest of the way."

She averts her gaze as I carry her up and to her bedroom. Once we get there, and I don't put her down, she looks at me expectantly.

The urge to kiss her almost overwhelms me, but she damn near leaps from my arms before I can try.

I haven't been with anyone, haven't even so much as kissed another girl since we broke up. I hung out with Lexie a few times but never allowed anything to get physical. It's not that I owed any loyalty to Evelyn. I just haven't had a desire for anyone else.

"What did you want to talk about?" Evelyn asks, interrupting my thoughts. She retrieves a hair tie and brings her mass of curls into a messy topknot.

"I was hoping you'd tell me the truth about everything. Why you went after my dad, the video ... everything."

She brings her full attention to me, and there's a level of discomfort behind her eyes. "Shepherd, I—"

"I know, it's not something you want to talk about, but for us to get past this, I have to know. Something hurt you. I don't know the half of it yet, but if you can let me in on some, it'll help me understand you more," I plead with her.

She takes a deep breath, looks at me intently, then sits on the bed. She gestures to me and I walk over without hesitation to sit next to her.

"It was for my brother," she says after a while.

When I look confused, she continues. "Do you remember when I told you about my brother, Ethan, who died?" I nod. "He was my twin, and he died in a car accident when we were eight."

Surprised, I gape at her. "I'm sorry."

"The man who caused the accident was acquitted. My brother was dead and no one, *no one* was punished for it."

I shake my head because I don't know what to say. The only thought I have now though is, what does this have to do with my dad? Was she implying he was the cause?

Ignoring me, she keeps going. "It came out in court that there was alcohol involved. Then all the evidence the prosecution had to that effect disappeared. I read up on it now that I'm older and mature enough to understand what happened with the case."

"So?"

"So? Your *dad*, Shepherd. It's clear to me now that he hasn't told you anything." She throws her hands up in frustration. "Your dad was the one driving the car that night. He was the one who had people conceal evidence. *He* was the one who was acquitted on vehicular manslaughter charges. He gets to enjoy his life, while my brother is dead!" Angry tears appear at the corners of her eyes, and she quickly swipes at them.

I remember being in a courthouse with my dad when I was little, but everything else is a blur. While I'm processing everything, she doesn't stop, doesn't give me a chance to react.

"When I saw your dad that night at the football game before homecoming, I wondered why he seemed so familiar. Then Tiffany told me who he was. You were such a jerk to me at that time, and I believed you were just like him. Then this plan, I don't know, came to me."

"What?" I ask, feeling gutted. "That you'd sleep with my dad to hurt me?"

"No! Of course not. I—" She rubs her hands against her dress. "Since he got out of the charges back then, I—I planned on getting him charged with ... something else.

Charges that he couldn't escape this time because the victim would be alive, and able to testify against him."

"So you were trying to get *my* dad to go to jail?" I try coming to terms with everything.

"Shepherd, it's not just that," she grinds out. "It's not, OK? This is about justice, righting the wrongs that were done to my brother, to my family. Why can't you see that?"

I stand because I'm starting to think she doesn't regret a thing she's done. "You apologized to me," I say, staring down into her dark eyes.

"What?" she asks in confusion.

"You said you were sorry for what you did. Was that a lie?"

"I said I was sorry for *using* you," she replies, getting up. "But I'm not sorry for wanting to put the murderer who killed my brother behind bars. It's where he belongs."

"You're talking about my dad, you know that right? And even though there's love lost between us sometimes, he's still my father." I stalk over to the window because I don't know how to feel at this point. I'm fighting with my girlfriend over my dad, again.

My *ex*-girlfriend.

"Well, if he was such a great dad, he wouldn't have hidden information about your mom trying to get into contact with you now would he?" She regrets saying the words because when I whip around to face her, she rushes into speech. "I was going to tell you, but the way I found out wasn't the best, so I never got the chance to explain—"

"What did you say?"

"That I was going to tell you but—"

"About my mother—what could you possibly know about my mother trying to contact me?" I narrow my eyes at her.

"Shepherd, she wanted to see you, but your dad kept it hidden," she says, her voice hesitant. "There's a silver case in his office desk that he keeps locked away." She pauses, watching me as I move to stand in front of her. "It has pictures of you and her together in it, and other stuff. I found a letter that had been ripped, but from what was left of it, she was trying to get your dad to let her see you. She knew some secret that he wanted hidden, but ...," she trails off.

"I'm sorry. Did you say she *wanted* my dad to let her see me?" I chuckle because the idea of that sounds so far-fetched, I can't believe it.

"Yes. She wanted to see you. It was written in that letter. But he obviously didn't let her."

"Evelyn, if my mother wanted to see me, she knew where our house was."

"That's the thing. From the letter, it seems she had something on him. Whatever it was, I feel like your dad was instrumental in making sure you never saw her again."

"Look, I know you hate my dad. But if you're trying to get me to side with some woman who abandoned her child to experience the shit I ended up experiencing, it's not going to work."

"I'm not trying to do anything except tell you the truth, Shepherd," she replies caustically.

"How convenient," I say, equally upset.

"What's that supposed to mean?" She sighs in frustration. "Look, you're the one who said you were ready to talk. If you don't believe me, check his office desk. There's a key under the top of it that opens the bottom drawer. That's where the silver case is."

"I'm not snooping through my dad's desk to prove whatever theory you think you know," I say, frowning down at her.

"Fine," she says, turning away from me to get something out of her dresser. She pulls out some clothes and walks over to the door of her bedroom. "We're done here. You don't believe a word I say, so I don't see the purpose of us continuing this conversation."

"Couldn't agree more." I brush past her and head out of the room and to the stairs. I'm about to go down them but turn back to find her still standing at the door of her bedroom.

She's staring at me, but when I see something akin to sadness in her eyes, I bite down hard and steel my emotions.

I turn and fly down the stairs. I don't want Evelyn's pity. I don't need her feeling sorry for me. My goal here tonight was for us to come to an understanding. I wanted her to be my girlfriend again.

I miss her.

I want her.

But I *refuse* to have her pity me.

Chapter Twenty-Six

SHEPHERD

I don't know what the hell I'm doing. It's been less than twenty-four hours since the bombshell Evelyn's dropped on me about my dad.

He's not here, but Jackie is. I'm waiting for her to leave so I can get into his office.

I can't believe I'm letting Evelyn get to me. But I have to do this. Even if it's for nothing more than to prove she's wrong about my dad.

As soon as Jackie opens the garage and pulls out and down the driveway, I run downstairs. I know my dad has cameras in his office but I don't give a shit.

After I unlock his office door I go straight to the desk, moving my hands under its surface. When I do, I come up with nothing.

"Damn it!"

I squat, looking under it as if by some miracle the key would somehow appear. I pull at his desk drawers. They all glide open. All except the last one on the bottom right.

I yank the shit out of it, hoping it'll give way. But it doesn't of course. I don't know if I'm crazed or just desperate, but I get a knife from the kitchen to see if I can pick the lock.

"Open up, you piece of shit!" I yell at the damned thing because obviously it'll listen and open because I cuss at it.

I'm working on the drawer, knife in one hand and now paper clip in the other, when I hear, "What exactly are you doing?"

I shoot up and find my dad standing at his office door, his eyes furious. "Why are you in here? And what are you doing over there?"

I stiffen, wanting to disappear into the walls. I didn't hear the garage, didn't hear the door.

"I asked you a question, Shepherd. What are you doing at my desk?"

At this point, I have no good response, at least nothing he'll like to hear, so I deflect. "I'm looking for stationery." Even to my ears this sounds like complete bullshit.

"With a knife and a paperclip?" he asks. "What do you plan on doing with the stationery? Slicing it up into pieces and putting it into a neat little stack?"

I look down at my hands. I hadn't realized I still held on to the tools.

Shit.

"Cut the crap and tell me what you're searching for."

I put the tools on his desk and inhale. "Dad, did my mother try to contact you after she left?" I go straight for the jugular.

His frown deepens. "I've already explained this to you," he replies, moving me out of the way to look at the drawer I was trying to get open. "I knew that girl wouldn't keep her mouth shut." He mumbles this to himself, then looks up at me. "Did she put you up to this?"

I take a good look at him. Then it dawns on me. The only reason he would assume Evelyn put me up to this is if he already knew she looked through the drawer. I remember his office cameras, and that's when I realize he's known all along that Evelyn snooped through it.

He stands to his full height in front of me and drags a hand down the planes of his face. When he turns to face me, something about the way he's looking at me half convinces me that he's about ready to lie. "Shepherd, look. Whatever that girl told you, it's not true. She's upset over some accident that occurred many years ago."

"Yeah, an accident that *killed* her brother." I don't like how he's trivializing the trauma Evelyn went through.

"Well, yes. Unfortunately, he didn't make it."

"I don't get why you're bringing that up anyway. What does the accident have to do with this drawer you don't want me gaining access to?" I emphasize my question by taking a booted foot to the drawer.

The stupid thing suddenly pushes out, opening before us.

We make eye contact.

I dive down to pull at the silver box peeking through under some photos. My hand catches air as Dad shoves me out of the way. He tries to push the drawer closed. But this must be some case of serendipity because try as he might, it refuses to close all the way.

I watch him struggle to lock it. "What're you hiding from me?" I demand.

He doesn't answer but continues fumbling with the drawer to get it closed.

"Dad, let me see what's in that silver case. I deserve to

know if my mom left us or if in fact *you* drove her away. What did she have on you?" When I say the words, he freezes.

The look he levels me when his eyes meet mine is cold, calculating. It's like he's trying to figure out the right words to shut me up about this whole thing. "Shepherd, it's not what you think. Your mother had an affair. She left because of her own selfish choices. She wasn't thinking of either of us—"

I don't even let him finish because if that's the truth, he'll let me see what's in the drawer. "Then let me see the case. Evelyn told me there were pictures of my mom and me in there. Let me see it, since I don't have many photos of her anyway." I dare him to refuse my request.

"You already have a picture. Why would you go through the added pain—"

"Let me decide if it's painful."

"No. I will not give you the case," he states, his demeanor unmoving.

"Then you've proved everything Evelyn said to me is true. You've been keeping my mother away from me. What does she know, Dad? And why didn't you tell me she wanted to see me? Where is she? I wanna see her." I'm angry because I'm aware now that I have even less of a dad than I thought I did.

"She's dead."

"No," I deny immediately. There's no way my mom is dead, no way.

"Yes, she is. She's dead to this family. Do you hear me!" he shouts, hate dripping from every angry word. He yanks the silver case from the drawer and tosses it into my arms.

I'm so shocked I almost drop it.

"Your mother doesn't have anything on me. She can't

touch me. But since you've already been told about that"—he points to the case in my hands—"go through it, toss it, burn it. It doesn't matter what you do with it. It's more trouble than it's worth holding on to it." He starts working to fix the drawer again.

I watch him, trying to figure out why he put up such a fight only to turn around and hand me the case.

"Is there something else, Shepherd?" he asks, eyes concentrated on what he's doing.

"No," I reply. I turn and walk to the door.

He heaves a long sigh before saying, "I did love your mother you know, and a part of me still does. But make no mistake, she tore this family apart, and for that, I don't think I'll ever be able to forgive her."

I continue walking, out of his office, down the hallway, then up to my room.

I don't know who or what to believe. With this case in my hands, I hope I'll be able to find some answers.

Chapter Twenty-Seven

SHEPHERD

I found out my mom has been in and out of rehab for drug and alcohol abuse for the past two years. She'd been clean for a few months but went back into another spiral. Reasons unknown to my dad, or so he says. I didn't push him for any more than the information I needed.

I'm in Atlanta for the weekend. I checked into a hotel close to the facilities my mom has been calling home for the better half of two years.

When my dad told me she's been this close to us the whole time, I didn't know how to feel. But then I thought about what a mess she's made of her life, and well, damn, I found myself feeling sorry for her.

"ID please." The woman at the front desk of the rehab facility takes my driver's license. She looks haggard, like she's spent most of the night fighting sleep. She tells me to wait while someone checks if my mom has been brought down.

I go to one of the unoccupied chairs in the waiting room, and as soon as I take a seat, I get a text.

Lucas is checking in.

I send him a quick update and let him know I'll fill him in after. He wanted to make the trip down with me for moral support, but I didn't want him here, in case things got too complicated.

"The patient is in waiting room three," the woman announces a few minutes later. "Go through that door, and wait in front of the second door on your right. They'll buzz you in." She offers a wan smile and directs her attention back to her computer screen.

I proceed to the path instructed. When I get to the second door on my right, I'm as stiff and unmoving as the metal it's made of.

There's a loud buzzing sound, but when I reach cold hands out to push in and enter the room, I hesitate.

What will I find when I get in there? Will she want to see me?

I push those questions out of my mind and focus on the night of the accident that took the life of Evelyn's brother. That was the catalyst for her hatred, and everything she did because of it.

Biting down on my own misgivings of what I could encounter, I push hard against the door, bursting into the room.

I freeze, rooted to the floor. The door closes behind me with a soft click, and I'm left staring at the woman who gave birth to me.

She's seated on a padded chair across a sterile metal table in the center of the room. She's petite, emaciated, and looks nothing like the beautiful woman of my memories. Her face is gaunt, with little semblance to the pictures I have of her. The once thick blonde hair is now a thin and dull version of its former glory.

She finally notices that someone is in the room with her.

I approach the chair in front of her on the other side of the table. Once seated, I don't speak at first. I steel my emotions, not knowing what to say.

"Shepherd?" she asks tentatively, her voice faint. "They told me my son was here to see me. I didn't believe it."

I still don't say anything. It's as if all the loathing I had pent up toward her faded the moment I saw her.

She reaches a timid hand across the table, placing it over mine. Her hand is ice, and I almost jump at the sensation of it against my skin.

"He's kept you from me for so long. You can't even recognize your own mother," she says in despair. Her other hand trembles as she raises it to wipe her eyes. Only there aren't any visible tears present.

"No," I hear myself respond, my voice firm. "I know who you are."

Whatever it is she sees on my face must give her pause because she immediately removes her hand from mine. "I knew he would poison you against me," she says angrily. "I should've run away with you when I had the chance. Look at how he's made you hate me. That sick son of a bitch." She continues spewing vitriol against Dad, and when she realizes her words aren't receiving the desired reaction, she stops. "Sorry. I know this all must be so hard for you to hear. Mike toots himself to you as some perfect father. But let me tell you, he's far from it."

For a woman who hasn't seen her son for so many years, this is what she chooses to lead with? Shouldn't she at least attempt to inquire after my well-being?

Of course, not her. She has too much anger and hatred for my dad to actually give a damn about me.

"How are you, Sheila?" I don't feel comfortable calling her *Mom*, and at this rate I don't think I ever will.

"Sheila?" she asks in exasperation. "You don't even see me as your mother, do you?"

The look I give her must convey my incredulity at the question.

She immediately backtracks. "I mean, I can understand that. I haven't been in your life much, but I'm not the one at fault for that," she argues.

Here we go again.

"It was your ridiculous father's decision to—"

"What happened the night of the accident? The night the little boy was killed?" I ask, interrupting her. I can see she's busy playing the victim with Dad, and it's going nowhere, fast. The concern I had for her when I first entered the room is fizzling out by the second.

She sits stumped for a moment, taken aback by the question.

I can see her mind working.

She narrows her gaze at me before asking, "Did Mike put you up to this? Why are you asking me about that night? What do you know about it?"

Her inquiry rids me of any doubts I may have had about Dad. "I'm asking because it's important to someone I love and care about," I admit honestly.

She continues eyeing me. "What's in it for me?" she demands, a sudden souring of her features changing any aspect of frailness I once saw there.

"What do you mean?" I fold my arms, curious.

"Well it's obvious you're not here out of concern for your poor institutionalized mother. So if you don't care that

I'm locked up here, then I have to look out for myself." She finishes in a huff, defensively crossing her sticklike arms.

"Oh really? And who's paying for your stay here?" I know at least that much. My dad bears that load. "Yeah, my dad. He's the one paying to get you out of this mess you got yourself in."

She brings her arms to her sides in defiance, then points an index finger at me. "I'm still your mother. Don't you dare take that tone with me."

How convenient.

"Will you let me know what happened, or ...?" I want to get this over with.

"How much are you willing to give me if I talk?" she persists.

Then I see it.

The selfishness. The absolute self-centered air about her. I'm not surprised. But a part of me thought that maybe we could've had a connection, some sort of mended relationship for the future. But Dad was right. This is a lost cause. *She* is a lost cause.

"How much do you want?" I don't care anymore. I'll get the money to her, however much she desires.

When she names her exorbitant price, I agree to it.

Like I said, I don't care.

Evelyn is worth more to me than money.

Chapter Twenty-Eight

EVIE

I have no classes with Shepherd this semester. I haven't seen him at lunch either. I haven't seen him since the day he came to my house after he got back from Colorado.

That's over two weeks ago.

I've texted him but barely got any responses. I don't know what to think. I know even less about what to do. But I do know what I feel.

I miss him.

I miss being around him, hanging out with him ...

I miss *us*. And I want him back.

I asked Jones how he's doing, and he just hinted that Shepherd was having a hard time with family stuff.

I'm on my way to my creative writing class when Beanca steps into my path.

I haven't forgotten that she was the one who invaded my privacy, causing the fallout with Shepherd. She was the one responsible for the whole video and posters fiasco.

I know she hates me. So wouldn't it be wise of her to avoid me altogether?

"What do you want?" I ask flatly. I have about five minutes before class starts and I don't plan on wasting them in conversation with her.

"You're honestly the worst thing to happen to Shepherd, do you know that?" she says, hatred evident in her green eyes.

At the mention of Shepherd's name, I focus on her words, hoping she'll continue.

"He hasn't been hanging out with any of us since the semester started. What the hell did you do to him? Huh? Lucas says he went to your place when he got back. What did you do?" She folds her arms out in front of her, eyebrows raised, waiting for my response.

"Not that it's anything to you, but I didn't *do* anything to him." I try to keep my composure, because damn, I didn't know Shepherd was avoiding his friends.

"You need to go fix it. I don't like him being like this. Yeah, he can be mad at me for my part in all this, but when it starts affecting his friendships with other people, I don't like it." I can tell she's worried about him, so I won't take offense at her telling me what I *need* to do.

"Thanks for letting me know," I say.

"That's it? That's all you have to say?" she asks, her eyes wide, with even more claws about ready to come out.

"Look, I'll talk to Shepherd. But don't talk to me like that. I've let you speak for long enough, and trust me, my patience is about right here," I reply, facing my palm toward the ground and lowering it to about mid-thigh.

"Ugh, whatever." She turns and stalks away.

I sigh heavily and pull out my phone to text Jones.

Me: Hey, could you do me a favor?

Jones: Sure, what's up?

After school's out, I have Jones take me up to Tallulah. It's a school night so I don't expect to spend the night here, but I feel like it's the best place for some alone time with Shepherd.

I had Jones call him and tell him that he had to get here quick. He made up some excuse to get Shepherd to come.

Jones stays with me until Shepherd pulls up, parking alongside us. It's a good thing Jones's car has super dark tints because I don't want to risk Shepherd seeing me, and getting upset that I'm up here with him. At least not before we get a chance to explain.

Shepherd gets out of his car, and my chest instantly expands at the sight of him. I frown though because it's cold out and all he has on are a T-shirt and sweats.

"Where's everybody?" he asks, closing his door and walking around to the hood of Jones's car.

I slink back into the darkness of Jones's car so he can't see me.

"Listen, Shep, I did this for you," Jones replies before coming to the back door.

Shepherd watches him warily as he opens the car door.

Once I step out, Shepherd's eyes flutter and widen in surprise as they take me in.

"The others aren't really coming for some urgent meeting. Evie wanted to talk to you. So I'll leave you two to it." Jones closes the back door, then gets in.

We both watch as he pulls out, leaving us there.

"What's this about?" Shepherd asks from behind me.

I turn to face him and notice he hasn't moved from the spot Jones left him in. "Aren't you cold? It's forty degrees out," I say, wrapping my scarf a little more snuggly around my neck.

"I don't know. Maybe I deserve to freeze," he replies, then looks at his car. He's left the engine running.

When his words register, alarm kicks in, and I direct my eyes to his. I walk over to him and grab hold of his hands. Bringing them to my mouth, I blow warm air against them. I can feel his eyes on me as I continue heating his cold hands.

"Let's get in the car," I tell him after a while. I keep hold of one of his hands, and walk us over to his car. Opening the back door, I get in and pull him in with me.

It's toasty in here, the seat warmers and heater apparently having been left on.

"Isn't this better?" I ask, moving a duffle bag he has on the back seat to the floor.

He doesn't respond but when I look over at him, he's staring at me. When his gaze drops to my lips, my breath hitches.

"I love that you have these again," he says distractedly, shifting his gaze to my hair. He brings a hand to the end of one of the twists and rolls it between his fingers.

I move over to sit closer to him and raise my hand to his forehead, brushing the curls back that had fallen over it in the wind.

"I'm sorry, Ev," he says quietly.

I pause, lowering my eyes to his. "What do you have to be sorry for? I'm the one who's sorry. For telling you about your mother the way I did, for—"

His lips are on mine within seconds, silencing me.

"Mmm, baby, I missed you," he rasps out between kisses. He unwraps my scarf, tossing it to the front seat. My jacket goes next.

I notice his hands are shaking, so I end the kiss. "Shepherd, are you still cold? You're shaking."

SHEPHERD

I have to tell her.

I reach for her, hold her face in my hands and kiss her again. I don't want to lose Evelyn. I want to stay like this, go back to the way it was before she did all this, before I found out about my family's involvement in her brother's death.

Evelyn covers my hands and breaks the kiss, gently pulling my trembling hands away from her face.

"Shepherd?" she asks, concern written all over her face.

"I just need you, Ev," I plead, attempting to pull at her sweater.

"No, Shepherd. Let's talk about what's going on." She takes my hands in hers, resting them in her lap. "Why've you been avoiding everybody?"

I'm nervous.

I know what I have to say but I don't want her looking at me any other way than she is now.

"What is it? What's wrong?" she asks, alarmed.

"I have something to tell you," I begin. "I just hope ..." I trail off because I don't even have the right to do that, to hope.

"OK, you're scaring me. Just tell me."

I lace our fingers together, and then look down at our joined hands. "The night of your brother's accident ..." I trail off again because I'm having a hard time getting the necessary words out.

"Yeah, what about it?"

"It wasn't my dad who ... caused his death."

The moment the words are out, she tries to pull her

hand free from mine, but I don't let her. "Let me go." She's agitated and averts her eyes to avoid looking at me. "It *was* your dad. I don't care how many lies he cooks up to try and convince you otherwise. You weren't there that night—"

"And you don't know the half of what happened yourself. You can't. You were only eight, Evelyn," I say firmly.

She vigorously tries to pull away from me, but I capture her in my arms. Her back to my chest, she's half sitting across my lap.

"Take me home," she says quietly, still continuing to struggle.

"I'm not finished," I reply firmly. "Don't you want to hear what I have left to say?"

"No."

I turn her to face me, holding both her hands in one of mine and gripping her chin in the other. "Ev, my *mother* was driving that night. My biological mother. Not my dad," I finally confess.

Her facial expression sours. "Is that what he told you? Of course, anything to avoid blame. Your dad's pinning this on her and refusing to own up to his criminal past! That's all." She tugs at her hands again.

"*No*. I looked into this myself, did the research myself, talked to my mother *myself*. It had nothing to do with him telling me anything. Actually, if it was up to him, I still wouldn't know any of this."

She's quiet for a long while.

I keep going. "The reason you found no evidence for the case is because my dad was acquitted. The evidence went to a different case with my biological mother as the plaintiff. They weren't together then, but that night, he'd taken her out of town. One thing led to another and they ended up in his car. She was the one driving. My dad, as lost as he was with the idea of getting her back, attempted to take the blame for the accident. He had her case buried as some last-ditch attempt at regaining her affection for him, but it didn't work. Look, I can admit my dad has his vices, some of them more disgusting than others. But he wasn't driving drunk that night, Evelyn, my mother was."

I give her time to process what I'm saying, but when she just sits there mute, it gets to me.

"Say something, please," I plead.

"Where's your mother now?" She asks the question in such a quiet voice, I struggle to make out what she said.

"She served time, about two years in jail before she was released early on good faith. She's been in Atlanta, in and out of rehab centers for the past two years."

I release her hands because of the tears that I see forming in her eyes, tears she doesn't want me to see. She turns her head away in embarrassment.

"I'm sorry." I feel like a jerk for having to unload on her like this.

"So"—she chuckles sarcastically—"what I did to you, to your dad, was really for nothing. I'm so *pathetic!*"

"Don't say that about yourself. You were hurting, and lashing out. How could you have known any of this?"

"I want to go home."

"Not right now, Ev. I think we should talk this out."

"What more is there to say, Shepherd?" She doesn't look at me but covers her face with her hands, shaking her head. "I don't even know how you can look at me right now. How could you even bare to touch me?"

"*Listen* to me," I say vehemently, turning her and forcing her to look me in the eyes. "My mother—I went to see her in person. She's worse than I thought, OK? She only cares about herself. How can someone who hasn't been in my life for the past twelve years ask me for money? After her second marriage didn't work out, she tried to blackmail my dad into giving her money. Even though he put his reputation and that of the family on the line for her, she still didn't care.

You two are *nothing* alike. You love your brother. You did this for him. Although I can't fully understand it, you weren't selfishly motivated."

She loses control of her emotions, letting the tears flow freely, not attempting to hide them from me anymore.

I instantly gather her into my arms.

She lets me.

"I was the one who thought you wouldn't want me near you after this," I add, gathering her more tightly against me when sobs rack her body.

"I—I could never—never want that," she admits between shaky breaths. Then she brings her arms up and around my shoulders, resting her head against me there.

We stay like that in the back seat of my car, Evelyn holding nothing back.

A while later, I kiss the scar on her neck, the one I know now to be from the night of the accident. We climb out and get in the front seats.

I start up the engine, placing an open palm on the console between us.

She slides her palm over mine, and we hold hands the entire journey home.

Chapter Twenty-Nine

SHEPHERD

"I want nothing to do with her," I admit. I tell Evelyn everything that happened during the visit with my mother.

She listens while looking at several family photos now present in her bedroom. Most of them include her brother.

She manages to school her features before facing me. "Don't let me or my family be the reason you don't have a relationship with your mom." She walks over, and reaching her hands up, she cradles my face. "That's not what I want for you. You mean more to me than that." She removes her hands then, covering her own face. When she finally looks up at me, I can see the unbridled hurt etching her features.

I immediately pull her into my arms. I don't like seeing her like this. It's like a soccer punch to the gut seeing her hurt.

"I blamed myself a lot," she whispers.

"What?" I ask, confused. "Babe, you had nothing to do—"

"Shepherd, I was the one who distracted my dad. And in that split second where he wasn't paying attention to the road, that's when it all happened." She shifts out of my embrace and moves to stand by one of the portraits perched on the nightstand by her window. "I mean, yeah, I took my anger out on your dad. But that was because of a promise I made to my brother. A part of me always felt my hands weren't completely clean in this."

"Evelyn, we were kids." I go over to her because there's no way I'll let her continue believing any of this is her fault. "None of this, and I mean none, was your fault or mine. The only person at fault here is my mother, and to some extent my dad, for letting her behind the wheel in the state she was in. And for that, I'm so sorry. If only for the fact that I'm her son."

At the first sign of tears behind her eyes, I reach for her, holding her again.

"I just wish he had a chance, you know," she struggles to get out between breaths. "I wish I had an opportunity to tell him I loved him, that I never hated him for a single second." She collapses into me, and we slide to the floor.

Her soft cries gut me.

"I love you, Ethan," she whispers, almost in despair. She continues repeating the phrase to herself.

I smooth my hand down her back, then run a thumb across her cheeks. "I love you, Evelyn," I whisper. I mean those words with everything in me.

When I notice she's gone quiet, almost completely still in my arms, I repeat them.

"Evelyn, I love you." I lower my head and place a kiss against first her forehead. "I love you." Then a tear-stained cheek. "I love you." Then her lips. "Babe, you're forgiven of whatever it is you think you've done wrong. You have to forgive yourself now." When she finally looks into my eyes, I continue, "Your brother loved you. And your parents do too. Nobody blames you for anything."

"Shepherd," she says, almost desperate, "my last words to him were 'I hate you.' There's no coming back from that!" she cries, covering her face again and shaking her head.

I pull her to my chest. "He knew you loved him, no matter what you said. It's in how you were with each other, what you did with, and for each other while you were together. I don't think for a second that he ever stopped loving you or believed those words you said in anger." I bring her face level with mine. "You need to forgive yourself."

She takes a slow, steady breath, looks up at the family portrait again, then returns her eyes to mine. Evelyn covers both my hands where I hold her face and leans over to kiss me. Hugging herself to me, she whispers, "Thank you for being here. Thank you for trying to make me feel better."

"It's not just about making you feel better, Evelyn. It's the truth."

She wipes at her tears with her palms, and when that doesn't work, she lifts up the edges of her blouse to dry them. "It's going to take some time for me to internalize what you've said as truth. You weren't there, and you aren't Ethan, so you don't know what he believed or didn't believe that night." She gets up, and out of my arms. "I appreciate what you're trying to do, but don't presume to think you know anything about my brother, or what he felt."

I don't respond. I stand up, then look down at her.

A few seconds pass.

"Stop looking at me like that," she says, an air of sadness mingled with irritation in her voice.

"Like what?"

"Like that. Like you're annoyed or upset with me."

I sigh in frustration because dealing with this side of Evelyn is taking a special kind of patience I didn't know I possessed. "Well, I attempted to tell my girlfriend the truth, and she basically tells me to stay out of her business. I don't know how exactly you want me to look at you, Evelyn."

"Fine," she says ruefully. "I'm sorry for making you feel that way. It wasn't my intention."

"Apology accepted," I reply.

I get it. I want Evelyn to be herself with me, even if it means I'll have to summon the patience of the saints to deal with whatever she dishes out.

She places a light peck against my lips.

I hug her to me. "On one condition," I add.

With narrowed eyes, she asks, "What's the condition?"

"You let me visit your brother's grave with you," I respond without hesitation.

When she stiffens in my arms, I feel like I've over-stepped again.

But she surprises me with her response. "Sure," she agrees, after some time. Relaxing against me, she raises her arms up and around my neck.

"For real?" I ask, genuinely shocked.

"Shepherd, don't make me change my mind."

I respond by lowering my head and sealing her lips to mine.

Chapter Thirty

EVIE

It took a lot for me to recognize that everything I did wasn't just about Ethan. My own hatred and resentment toward Mr. Buchanan created a mountain of emotions, which caused me to make some of the worst decisions of my life.

I almost ruined my relationship with Shepherd, a relationship that has come to mean more to me than I ever thought possible.

I will always love my brother, always cherish the memories I have. But I can't allow that tragic evening to color my future or influence the choices I make. Ethan wouldn't want that. He'd probably make fun of me for being such a big baby, who still didn't like trying certain things.

"So, what'll it be?" our waitress asks, standing with notepad in hand. She's not too friendly but does enough to ensure she makes a decent tip from our tables.

A large group of us are out celebrating the end of the school year.

"We'll have a large order of your sake, with the three variety rolls combo," Shepherd says before looking over at me. "Ev, are you good with the salad? Or?" He looks regretful.

We're at the same Japanese joint Jones took Tiffany and me to earlier in the year. We didn't have a choice where the group decided to eat for tonight, but I didn't want to miss out.

"I actually want to try the sake. It looks pretty good," I say.

Shepherd doesn't respond for a good couple of seconds.

"What?" I ask, curious to know what he's thinking.

"Are you sure? I mean, you don't have to if it makes you think of him."

Shepherd is the best person I know. He has this kindness streak in him most people don't know he possesses. It's the part of him I love most.

"I'm sure, babe. I can't think of anyone else that I'd rather experience this with." I reach a palm up to his face and pull him in for a kiss.

"Ugh. Get a room, you two," Lucas groans on the other side of the booth behind us.

"Shut up, bro," Shepherd replies, chucking Lucas in the shoulder over the seat. "Don't be mad 'cause Michelle decided to sit this one out."

"Ohhhhh," a group of players hoot in unison.

"Whatever, dude," Lucas counters, "I'm seeing her tonight anyway."

The rest of the guys start making whistling noises and the loud chatter in the room continues.

Lucas gets up and comes to stand beside our table. "Shep, have you seen the chat? Jones isn't coming tonight. Says he has other plans."

"That's weird. Last I checked, he didn't have any other plans." Shepherd frowns, then looks over at me.

I hold my hands up. "Don't look at me. I don't know anything."

"You know how he can get private when it's something he thinks he can't completely trust us with. I swear, are we even best friends?" Lucas sighs. "Whatever, I bet it's some girl." He goes back to his seat.

Shepherd immediately brings his hard gaze back to mine. "Are you sure you don't know anything about what's going on with Jones?"

"Babe, I wouldn't lie to you. Especially now, and about something like this." We've come too far for that. We've hiked Mount Kilimanjaro in our relationship already, and I'm not ready for Everest. I wouldn't keep anything from Shepherd, least of all something about Jones.

"You're right." He sighs. "Jones and I don't talk as much anymore, and now he won't even tell Lucas or Beanca anything. Not that I'd know if he did tell Beanca."

OK, well this is where I shut up because there's nothing I'd rather talk less about than the subject of Beanca Carlyle. If she had it her way, the relationship between Shepherd and me would be worse than that of the Montagues and the Capulets.

"Let's change the subject. How about that road trip you've been asking me about?" I say, bright-eyed because my parents finally gave me the green light.

Shepherd's eyes go wide, and his grin is the sun. "What'd they say?" he asks.

"They said yes," I reply, eager.

"Seriously?" He plants a hard kiss on my lips. "Yaasss! We're on one this summer," he groans out.

"There's a catch, though," I add. "My dad says we need

to check in with them at least twice a day, and no going anywhere further than the tristate area."

"I'm not mad at that," he says, then whispers in my ear, "I love you."

I cup my hands around his ear and whisper, "I love you, too. Forever." And I mean every single word.

I'm looking forward to this summer.

Nothing but the wind at our backs, and the brightness of the sun to always lead us forward.

A Poem for Ethan

Ethan,

It's over
You are free
I know that you've forgiven me
So now I'm free too
I love you
No matter what
I said that night
You were always an important light
In my life
Fly, Ethan
I'm releasing you
May you forever be the you
That I know and treasure
Above all measure
Things you loved
Things you liked
Big or small
I'll honor them all

Embers of Hate

I'll enjoy everything on your behalf
You were always my other half
With that said, I confess
I met someone through this mess
I made
In a way, it seems you lead
Us to each other
He's made me better
And guess what?
Tell you a little secret?
Sushi isn't so bad after all

Your twin,
Evie

Sneak Peek: PSA Book 2
"Fractured Redemption"
Lucas & Beanca's Story

BEANCA

Parents aren't supposed to play favorites.

They aren't supposed to treat one child like the prodigy and the other like the black sheep.

Key words there are "aren't supposed to."

I guess mine happened to have skipped out on that lesson.

"Beanca, you are so forgetful. I swear most of the time you only have one neuron bouncing around in your head." Dad heaves a sigh, picks his cell phone up from the kitchen counter and dials Mom.

"Honey, will you pick up Beverly? Beanca forgot she was coming home today."

My sister, Beverly, is coming back from cheer camp.

She didn't make our school's cheerleading team, so Mom and Dad thought it a good idea to send her to Tisch Cheer Camp up in Wisconsin for the summer. She's been gone for the past six weeks.

We go to Paramount School of Arts together. This

upcoming year will be my senior year and Beverly will be a sophomore.

Twirling my ponytail around my fingers, I try to ignore Dad's insult as I stride into the study.

I truly forgot my sister would be coming home today, but it wasn't my fault. I've had a lot on my plate. I volunteer with the Boys and Girls club in Paramount, and I'm also involved in PSA's Reading Rangers, an organization that pairs high schoolers with kids in middle school and elementary school who struggle with reading. Throughout the summer I've been enjoying the time I spend working with different groups of kids. I especially liked helping the struggling readers. I feel connected to them in some way. For one thing, we share the lack of parental support and devotion in our development, so I guess I have a vested interest in wanting to see them succeed.

If Dad had reminded me that Beverly was supposed to come home today, it would have fixed the current dilemma. If he cared to talk to me at all, instead of always criticizing me, maybe this wouldn't have happened.

I glide my hand across one of the many shelves of books that line the four walls of the study.

This is my favorite place in our house. Well, besides my bedroom. I could lose myself in here, spending hours engrossed in one of the volumes. I crook my finger when my hand reaches the book I'm currently interested in starting, *The Alchemist.*

Lucas recommended it.

He's one of my best friends.

There are four of us in our little circle. But, it's been more of a trio lately since Shepherd, our fourth man standing, decided he wanted nothing to do with me. I get it, I was a bitch to his girlfriend and almost ruined their relationship.

But seriously, I was only trying to help. And only because I cared about him. I'm hoping one day he'll see it and forgive me for the shady way I went about everything.

After reading almost half of part one of *The Alchemist*, I'm hooked. I want to keep going but I need to practice for my recital. I slide out of the loveseat and go over to my next favorite thing in this room, the piano. My parents never doted on me, and if they hadn't bought this for the prestige and aesthetic it brought to this house, I doubt they'd have purchased it had I asked them crawling on my knees over broken glass.

It wasn't always like this with them. There was a time when they loved both Beverly and me equally. As equally as parents can love two very different children anyway.

Things started changing around my seventh birthday. I'd had a nasty fall from one of the trees in our backyard. I'd broken my arm and had suffered an awful concussion. When I'd finally woken up, I'd noticed my dad acting distant, almost like I was a stranger to him. I'd chalked it up to him having been scared shitless that I could have died. But his behavior didn't return to normal. After a few months, my mom had changed toward me too. She definitely wasn't as bad as my dad, but it had been evident that her affection for me had waned considerably.

Beverly became the prized princess at our house. The venerable queen bee. She could do no wrong. So anytime something occurred that wasn't to my parents' liking, I was always the one to blame. And anytime something praiseworthy happened, they'd find a way to commend Beverly, even if it was clear I'd accomplished it. For example, if I'd get straight As, they'd say Beverly's study habits must have rubbed off on me. If I'd start helping around the house, with small tasks the maids didn't finish, they'd say Beverly must have been the one to do it because I was too selfish to think of anyone else.

If I'm selfish, it's because I've realized for a while now that I'm not lovable. People's affection for me never lasts. They always end up finding someone more deserving. Even when I'd tried being more like Beverly, acting like her, copying her style, attempting to imitate her personality, nothing ever worked.

I love my sister.

I only wish we were born to two different families. That way she could occupy a space where she received her own affection, and I would have mine. Two parents actually loving me, seeing me, spending time with me.

My fingers glide across the keys of the piano, and the notes of Prelude in E minor by Chopin fill the room. I close my eyes, feeling the music.

I play the piece over and over again, as I let the inevitable tears flow. They fall on my hands, on my lap, on the keys of the piano.

I can't stop them. They've become me in this house.

One more year.

Just one more year and I'll be out of here.

I should be happy about that.

I tell myself I *am* happy about it.

Maybe if I tell myself enough times, I'll eventually feel it.

LUCAS

"Hey, let's change the note here. E minor would give a more emotional effect," I suggest, stopping mid-song and switching to said chord on my guitar.

"Dude, we don't want the lower notes to overpower the

song too much though," Ricardo, one of the bass guitarists, chimes in.

"I'm with Lucas. The E minor makes the most sense here." Michelle is our lead singer and she'll be carrying the song, so what she says holds a lot of weight.

We're a small group in a larger club, the Paramount School of Arts music club to be exact. We've been practicing together over the summer and have written a few songs in preparation for our senior showcase at the end of the fall semester.

When it comes to music, this is where I geek out.

I'm a football player on PSA's varsity team, and although that's been a big part of my life, music is my core, my foundation.

"Could we speed up the chorus? And play harder when it gets to the end of it. That way it'll make for a deeper contrast with the softer, slower second verse," Michelle says.

We make the necessary changes and after about an hour, the song is thoroughly fleshed out. At least for today. With only one week left before school starts we wanted to get at least four more sessions in. I need those because I don't want to have to choose between football and my music.

I have a strong feeling it'll come down to that this year.

My phone vibrates as I place my guitar in its case. I pull it out of my pocket and look at the caller ID.

Oh great.

It's only 9 p.m., it's too early for this.

"Yeah, this is Lucas. I'm on my way." I don't even give the guy on the line a chance to explain. "Hey, I'm out. See y'all tomorrow."

"Later, Luke," I hear Michelle call back to me.

I turn, walking backward and waving at her. She smiles and I answer her with one of my own.

When I get to my truck, I throw my guitar on the back seat and climb in. I back out of Ricardo's driveway and head straight to Lilac Alehouse twenty minutes across town.

I make it there in ten.

When I get inside, the owner spots me and gestures over to where she's slumped over on one of the stools at the bar.

She is my mother, Laura Moore. She had me when she was a teenager and married my dad not too long after she'd found out she was pregnant with me. His family is super traditional, so even though they hadn't been in love, they'd been *encouraged* to marry.

Anyway, my dad died a few years back of a drug overdose so I don't touch that stuff, *ever*. I've read up on it and I'm aware that based on my background, I had the propensity to abuse it.

My mom, on the other hand, never had an alcohol abuse problem until she lost her position at her company last year. She was a supervising manager, and some case with an important client went sour. He'd threatened to pull out if she wasn't released from her duties, and of course the company chose him over her. It wasn't like either of us had to work. I'd inherited enough money to take care of the both of us for the next two lifetimes. But that didn't matter to her. She always prided herself on being an independent woman. So when my dad had suggested she not work, she'd still insisted on it.

I get to her and place one of her arms over my shoulder. "Come on, Mom, let's go."

"He ... ruined me," she slurs. She reeks of vodka, her breath, her clothes. "That man, he—he's making my life ... hell. Lucas—"

She stops up short as I open the passenger side door of my truck and start lifting her in.

"Nooooo," she groans. "I don't want … to go home."

I ignore her protests as I place her down gently on the seat and buckle her in. I swing around to the other side and drive away from the bar. I don't bother trying to give my mom a lecture because she won't listen or hear it for that matter in the state she's in right now. I've tried asking her to see a specialist, a therapist, someone, *anyone* who could help her. This habit of drinking herself into oblivion has gotten out of control at this point. I don't want her ending up like Dad.

It wasn't that I didn't grieve the loss of my dad, I did. We didn't have a super close relationship, since he was always gone on one trip or another. He provided for his wife and his child, and to him that's what it had meant to be a father. I hadn't complained, I had my friends and I knew he loved me in his own way. That had been enough for me.

When he died, I took over the helm as the man of the house.

I take care of my mom, and even though sometimes it can get stressful, like tonight when I have to go collect her from Lilac's, I accept the responsibility of seeing she's alright.

But she hasn't been, especially in the past two months. I admit that the alcohol abuse problem has gotten out of hand. I'll hire a professional who can make house visits because I know my mother won't leave this house to see anyone. At least no one but that bartender who'd gladly hand her the next drink.

I click open the wrought iron gates that stretch to about twelve feet high, and drive around to the entrance of our massive two-story house. It's been in my family for the past five generations and its Gothic architecture makes it look like something straight out of the *Addams Family.*

I park my truck in the circular driveway and as soon as I get to my mother, Keenan is there to lift her out. He's one of the guys we hired on as a live-in groundskeeper.

"Good evening, Keenan. You know where to take her," I say, closing my truck and falling into step behind them. We enter the house and he brings her up to her room located in the east wing. He's trustworthy, so I'm never worried about leaving him alone with her.

I go to my dad's former study. I immediately pick up the receiver to call our secretary. Yeah, we have one of those. Well Mrs. McCall was formerly my father's secretary so we kept her on to handle our family's affairs.

"Good evening, Mr. Moore. To what do I owe this phone call so late in the evening?" she asks, and I can detect the slight annoyance in her voice.

I hadn't paid attention to the fact that it was almost ten o'clock. "I'm sorry, Mrs. McCall, but I need you to find a professional who's able to help my mom."

Her annoyance is instantly replaced with genuine concern. "Oh dear. Did it happen again tonight?"

"Yeah, and I don't think I'm equipped to affect any sort of change anymore."

"OK. You don't worry yourself, young man. I should have someone for you before the day is out tomorrow." We hang up, and a sense of temporary relief washes over me.

I head up to my room on the opposite side of the house. Stripping down, I step into the shower. As the warm water pours over me, I think about the prospect of moving into one of the rooms on my mom's side of the house, just so I can monitor her more easily. I'm the kid, but I'd fast had to become the parent for my parent. Life sure knows how to throw curveballs.

I think about what my mother said tonight, about some guy who's trying to ruin her life, and I make a mental note to ask her about that when she's sober.

My mind calms a bit as the water soothes and relaxes my muscles. A lyric comes to me and I make marks in one of the fogged-up sliding doors of the shower.

As soon as I get out, I wrap a towel around my waist and head across the hall to my bedroom. I grab my notepad and jot down the words, along with the notes that accompany them.

> *With you by my side, pretty girl,*
> *We're up for a wild ride*
> *Cause the downs of this life*
> *With you as my wife*

I immediately pause and scratch out the last line, because what the hell?

I shake my head and send a few ringlets of water splashing against the page. I place the notepad on my bed and reach for my guitar.

Damn.

I left it in the truck.

The system signals movement at the front door, so I go over to look at the intercom. Beanca's face is on the screen. I'm not surprised she's here this late; she'll likely be staying the night. For the life of me, I can't understand how the hell her parents let her stay out this late or over at friends' houses so often. My mom hates it when I'm not home, especially on nights like this when she's been drinking.

I push the button that unlocks the front door to allow

her in, then I press on the speaker, "Hey, Bee, could you go over to my truck? I left my guitar on the back seat."

"*Lu-cas*," she groans. She rolls her eyes and then heads in the direction of where my truck's parked.

I grin as I watch her open the back door and retrieve the case. I'm about to head downstairs to meet her, when I remember that I'm only in a towel. I throw on a pair of sweatpants, not bothering with a shirt, then exit my room.

"Why is this thing so heavy?" she asks as she hands the case over to me. "And where is the rest of your clothes?"

"My house, remember, my rules. I'm allowed to be in any state of undress. You're lucky I even have these on," I tease, gesturing to my sweatpants.

"Ugh, you're so gross. I can't even." She steps past me and takes her long blonde hair out of its customary ponytail. Her hair falls to her back, almost reaching her waist. Staring at it, I walk past her and tug on a few strands. She winces in pain, but I know it's a pretense when she continues talking. "So I started *The Alchemist*."

I immediately swing around to face her. "Seriously? How far'd you get?" I told her about the book a couple of days ago when I'd gotten through reading it. I'd recommended it to her, Jones, and Shepherd.

Shepherd's one of our best friends. I know he hasn't gotten to reading the book yet. He and his girlfriend, Evie, have been on a road trip for the better half of summer. Their social media feed is full of pictures of all the cities they've visited. I'm not going to lie, I felt a little jealous, but I had to stay in Paramount this summer to get shit done. Jones, our other best friend, is still in Baltimore. Most of his family lives there, so he went for summer vacation and won't be back until school starts next week.

"I read most of part one. I think it's one of the best books

I've read recently and that's saying a lot since I'm not even finished." Beanca's gaze shifts to my chest, then back up to my face. When she catches me grinning at her, she rolls her eyes and reiterates, "Put a shirt on, Lucas."

I wriggle my eyebrows at her, "See something you like, Bee?"

"Oh, shut up. As if."

Acknowledgments

My mother who supports me in everything I do. My sister for being my sounding board for the stories always bouncing around in my head. My friends who help shape my writing with their insights.

About the Author

Sasha-Marie Marshall is an emerging author. *Embers of Hate* is her debut YA novel. She made the leap from years in education to author of inspirational novels and existing in the eternal now, living out her dreams one story and one endeavor at a time.

She currently resides in the USA, but being an avid traveler, she looks forward to her next adventure.

To keep updated on her upcoming releases, sneak peeks and extras, you can sign up to her email list at her website here: www.sashamariemarshall.com

www.ingramcontent.com/pod-product-compliance
Lightning Source LLC
Chambersburg PA
CBHW061229310726
48971CB00007B/1993